Cristina Jurado is a bilir  fantasy, horror and otl editor, translator and sf the first female author Award (Spain's Hugo) for *Bionautas.* ___ in English includes the translation of *Bionautas* (Twine), and many stories in various venues, such as *Strange Horizons*, *Clarkesworld* and *Apex Magazine*, as well as *The Best of World SF* by Head of Zeus. Her works have been translated into Italian, Romanian, Chinese and Japanese.

As editor she has published several books: *Alucinadas*, the first anthology of sf short stories written by women in Spanish (translated into English as *Spanish Women of Wonder*); *Infiltradas*, the first anthology in Peninsular Spain of feminist sf articles, which won the Best Non-Fiction Book Ignotus Award in 2020; and *Todos los demás planetas*, an sf anthology focused on inclusive language. In 2015 Cristina founded *SuperSonic*, winner of three Best Magazine Ignotus Awards and honoured by the European Science Fiction association (ESFS) as Best Zine in 2016 and Best Magazine in 2017. She has worked as international editor for *Apex Magazine* and has co-edited, with Lavie Tidhar, *The Apex Book of World SF #5*, focused on speculative fiction around the world. She currently works as co-editor for Futura House, a blog featuring stories from Hispanic authors in English.

Distinguished as Europe's Best SF Promoter Award in 2020, she has worked as editor and contributor for *Apex Magazine* and *Constelación* magazine, and as Spanish slush reader for *Clarkesworld*.

'Cristina Jurado is a powerful new voice in Spanish speculative fiction'

Lavie Tidhar, 2017 John W. Campbell Award Winner for *Central Station* and 2011 World Fantasy Award for *Osama*

'Here is erotic cosmic dark fantasy; here is a doomed astronaut snatched from suicide in space by ... something. Here is a psychopath with her memories erased, murderously on the trail of Who, and Why? Here are very dark visceral visions—of a swamp creature upon the ceiling, of ruthless bestial battles against shadows. Here are radically "other" stories, muscular, gritty, evocative. Here's your chance to relish what Spanish readers voted the best story of 2017. I am so impressed by this outstanding, and eloquently translated, collection.'

Ian Watson, author of the screen story for Steven Spielberg's *A.I. Artificial Intelligence*

'Jurado's fiction sometimes defies classification, but is always stimulating, imaginative and thought-provoking. Thank the stars that none of the quality got lost in translation. Any fan of fantastical fiction will enjoy the stories in *Alphaland*'

Tade Thompson, author of *Rosewater* and *The Murders of Molly Southbourne*

'Stories of identity, paranoia and loss that resonate in the mind and which will leave you both uncomfortable and entertained. Recommended for any fan of dark fiction.'

Jason Sizemore, Hugo-nominated editor of Apex Publications

Alphaland
AND OTHER TALES

CALQUE PRESS

.

ALPHALAND
AND OTHER TALES

CRISTINA JURADO

Prior publications: 'Embracing the movement', *Clarkesworld*, issue 177, June 2021; 'Lamia', *Apex magazine*, February 2022; 'Dump', *Best of World SF, vol. 1* (ed. Lavie Tidhar, Head of Zeus 2021)

All stories © Cristina Jurado 2023.
Translations: 'Vanth', 'Inchworm', 'Second Death of the Father', 'The Shepherd' © James Womack 2017. 'Embracing the movement' © Sue Burke 2021. 'Lamia' © Monica Louzon 2022. 'Dump' © Steve Redwood 2020. 'Short Fiction as the Seedbed of Speculative Fiction' ©Inés Galiano 2022.

Introduction © Robert Shearman 2023
Cover design © Vince Haig 2023
Edited and Typeset by Calque Press
Proofreading by Dan Coxon
http://calquepress.com
ISBN: 978-1-9162321-6-7
Type: Hoefler Text
British Library Cataloguing-in-Publication Data
A catalogue record for this book is available from the British Library
Calque Press
An Imprint of Nevsky Editions Ltd.
2023

All plausible efforts have been made to contact the copyright holders of translations in this volume. Please contact the publisher if you notice or are aware of any omissions; they will be happy to make acknowledgement in future editions.

All rights reserved. This book is sold subject to the condition that it shall not, by way of trade or otherwise, be lent, re-sold, hired out or otherwise circulated without the publisher's prior consent in any form of binding or cover other than that in which it is published and without a similar condition including this condition being imposed on the subsequent publisher.

CONTENTS

INTRODUCTION

I FELL IN LOVE WITH CRISTINA JURADO'S STORIES AT thirty thousand feet. I'd been attending a writer conference in Barcelona and had agreed to appear on a panel discussing the short story. It was, I think, quite a difficult panel—more theoretical and intellectual than any I was used to in Britain, where writers tend to shy away from analysing the craft of what we do and instead hide behind jokes. There were (I'm remembering?) eight writers on the panel: Spanish, English, French, all talking in our own languages, our questions being simultaneously translated in earpieces, our answers being simultaneously translated back and boomed out to the audience. It was moderated by Cristina Jurado, and I was impressed by the way she cheerfully juggled all the different nationalities and creative disciplines and vast egos competing for attention, to produce an event that was not only coherent but entertaining and revealing.

I was the least renowned writer on the panel—as the old joke goes, the only one there I had never heard of. And I was frightened that with every word I spoke (in English), and every word the audience heard (in Spanish), I was testing everyone's patience, not least Cristina Jurado's, who seemed to listen to my answers with a solemn respect I guessed she knew they did not deserve. I decided that if I could get through the panel maintaining her respect—and her respect alone, never mind my fellow writers, never mind that audience—that I could claim the whole thing as a victory. After it was all over, and one by one the combined nations of Europe shuffled off the stage, I dared approach her. I thought I would be able to read on her face the exact level of tolerant politeness to gauge how bad I'd been. Cristina wasn't tolerant at all. Nor was she polite. Instead, she beamed at me, and asked if she could give me a hug—she told me she'd long known my work and enjoyed it, and had been so looking forward to meeting me. I was so touched (and so relieved)—it was such a generous thing to say—and I decided immediately that at least I could return the favour and get to know her work too. That evening in my hotel room I downloaded a collection of her short stories on to my kindle.

And yet it was only when flying back home to London that I found time to read them. I had eaten my complimentary peanuts and drunk my complimentary orange juice. I had looked at the clouds for as long as the clouds could bear it—there was a whole sea of them outside my window, and they looked very beautiful, but I could now conclude they weren't going to do anything. And I wondered why I was suddenly so reluctant to read Cristina's stories—because I was, somehow, wasn't I? I think it was because I had been genuinely in awe of her when we had been together on stage, and sincerely impressed that she had any liking for my own work—she was kind and witty and very clever and I instinctively knew she'd be good, but up here in the clouds, it felt tempting not to have to be confronted by the reality of what that might mean. Not that I feared disappointment—it's hard to explain—more that I feared, I suppose, that reading the stories would inevitably turn them into just that, stories, words upon the page that were neat and contained, and it would be so easy to leave them unread as unknowable possibilities. Self-indulgent of me, and stupid, and actually rather unkind. I pulled myself together. No, I would read one story, just one. It would be a poor return on her generosity towards me, but then I'd know at least a smidgen of what she wrote—and by the time I finished maybe there would be more peanuts to eat, more clouds to watch. I turned on my kindle. The book was called *Alphaland*. (In slightly truncated form—the version you are reading now is a new, expanded edition.) The first story was called 'Vanth'. I began to read it.

13

I was shocked by 'Vanth'. It hadn't been what I was expecting at all. Because what Cristina Jurado had demonstrated on stage was order and patience—and here was this story, and it was a whirlwind blast of insanity—something that knew what order was and understood order very well thank you and wanted to tear order down and stamp upon it—something that had given up on patience and instead wanted to howl. I did for a moment wondered whether I regretted reading it after all—but not for the reasons I feared, because this was a story that felt anything but neat and contained, it seemed to bleed out of its confines somehow. I knew it was one of those very rare stories that come into your life that challenge your understanding of reality, and leave their mark upon you. It is a horror story, yes. But not in the usual fashion of horror. This is a tale that pulls you close just as it appears to repel you, it seduces you by gently whispering the most terrible things into your ear. I didn't know how to respond to it—and I think that was the breathtaking joy of it, too, that 'Vanth' didn't need to care how I responded. It was bigger and more beautiful than that. It was only as I finished the final paragraph that I realised I'd been holding my breath for a long time, I was so tense. I had the instinct to hide my kindle away. I had another instinct to go back, read the same story, read it over again. That's the instinct that won. I wanted to see if I could work out how Jurado had managed to pull off that extraordinary balancing act between disgust and desire.

Then I looked out of the window again for a while, and that sea of clouds seemed to have twisted themselves into strange grotesque shapes, looping themselves and through each other. They looked impossible. I turned back to Cristina Jurado. I read her next story. And then the next. And the next. I was, indeed, offered more peanuts; I refused.

Cristina Jurado challenges the senses. It's comparatively easy for a writer to play on sensory deprivation—create a state where both character and reader feel blinded, or deafened, or mute. It is just a little harder, I think, to expand those senses, so that for a brief spell on the page you're given a more acute sight or touch through thick description and introspect. Jurado never does anything quite so simple. Instead she writes of people who are in the process of transition— even of bodily mutation—passing from one set of senses to something dangerous and extreme and strange. She writes of impossible imaginings with clinical, real precision—the way that during death senses are both blunted and yet exploded in glorious, contradictory ways—the way that as the flesh transcends the structural limits of the body it introduces ecstasies of agony and delight outside rational experience. And she makes these impossible senses beautifully credible— emphatically credible. Time and time again Jurado examines what it is like for us to be human beings, and then to transform us into something new.

For these are tales of transformation. Of people into monsters, into dead things, into things more alive than they could ever have guessed possible—into infinite extensions of flesh stretched out fine like chewing gum. Of women into fathers, and men into women, and men into machines. And all done with such wonder—and if there is fear, then it's the human fear of the unknown, not of the pain that might be suffered in the process—because there is nothing cruel or sadistic about Jurado's writing, even as she wraps her characters up into gruesome shapes. Jurado's characters exist in the moments of glory before they lose their identities—their fates are frightening and disturbing, but at the same time fascinating, and even arousing. You find yourself longing to be the victim of a Jurado story—to be brave enough to be lost forever within her imagination.

And I'm drawn back to that generosity I saw in Cristina Jurado when I met her—because there is an unusual generosity to her strange tales. 'Vanth' could very easily have been the story of a boorish, abusive man, and the exquisite comeuppance he deserves. But it is prefaced by a tender and realistic piece of writing, almost a short story of its own, about a little boy suffering at the expectations of what it is to be masculine, taking pains to explore the psychology of the monster, giving him a context for his macho misogyny without apologising for it. Everyone feels rooted to a world that has real gravity, no matter how alien their final destination—these are people composed of true memories, of subtle regrets and poignant joys.

It's that, I think, that gives such power to the changes wrought in these tales. As the characters give up the burden of who they are, you are presented with exactly what is being lost—and, as a result, what is being gained. The world that they are required to sacrifice may be harsher and meaner and plainer than the disquieting unknowns ahead—even if those unknowns might be the utter obliteration of their own selves.

And I love Jurado's stories because they play always with my expectations both of horror, and the short story in general. The short story is always about change—often, small delicate events that prove cataclysmic. Jurado leans into the yawning abyss of the cataclysm—and, daringly, invites us to embrace it. Nothing is ever quite permanent in her worlds—you can reinvent yourself there, and if you resist that opportunity, then something may come along and do the reinventing for you. There's a dark eroticism to this—she holds up the mirrors to our selves, then distorts the reflection, and then makes us long to be distorted as well. It's why her stories seem truly transgressive, that the narrator never sits in judgment over her characters, or, more crucially, her readers' responses to them: neither offering comfort or sentiment, Jurado instead presents her tales of crumbling realities and madness with the air of a detached clinician. She seduces you without ever appearing to beg for your affection. She leads you into dark places without needing to turn her head to see if you're following behind. She already knows you are.

This is what I discovered, reading Cristina Jurado's stories for the first time, being lured into her imagination, looking out of my aeroplane window at that sea of chopped cloud which broke into slivers of dizzying space. That each story moved me—shockingly, quite intensely—and it was the unexpectedness of it, that in no way do the tales ever seek to provide a pat emotional resolution, that moved me all the more. These are stories of revenge without the expected *Schadenfreude*, tales of love without the expected clichés, tales of new worlds without the expected awe: instead Jurado ushers you into a luminal state where you can no longer be entirely sure of what you know or what you feel: wisps of cloud that look substantial enough for me to walk on, but would have me plummet into freefall if I tried. But oh!—what would that fall feel like, how exciting, how daring, how new. Something beautiful and terrifying all at once.

Robert Shearman

ALPHALAND
AND OTHER TALES

VANTH

Because there was only one thing worse than dying. And that was knowing you were going to die. And where. And how.

Richard Matheson, 'Death Ship'

CONDEMNED MEN HAVE THE PRIVILEGE OF KNOWING when their last day dawns. For the rest, there are no signs that announce it, no omens that establish the precise spatio-temporal coordinates of their demise. There is no warning. Not even terminal disease or perilous circumstance allows us to tell precisely at what moment the heart will seize up and the blood will start to cool. There are only presentiments which try to predict this moment, anomalies in one's memory that act like a feedback loop, suggesting that this entirely new experience is also one that we remember.

There is a kid in the middle of a dark forest, in a reserve on the Madrid *sierra*. He's not really a child; rather he exists in that indeterminate land between childhood and adolescence.

He has been sitting there since dawn, waiting; sitting with a group of men who are more than three times his age. All of them are smoking, their teeth yellow with nicotine. Some of them have yellow eyes as well, and their hands shake. The kid knows that it is not from the cold or from fear of the vermin they are here to destroy, because the hunters are safely in the shelter of their hides, protected by their fur coats. They tremble because of the booze in their hipflasks, the visible manifestation of their alcoholism.

It is most visible in his father, who has been a drinker for a long time now. Sometimes the child is afraid that his father is going to go into convulsions, because the shaking goes up his arms, all the way to his shoulders. He looks like one of those dolls with a large head mounted on springs, the ones people put on their dashboards and watch shake along to the rhythms of the car. Except in this case it is the body that shakes uncontrollably.

'He works a lot,' his mother says when she wakes the boy up before dawn every Sunday. 'Hunting takes his mind off things. It'll be good for you to spend some time with him alone, just the two of you, just you men.'

The boy says nothing; he knows he doesn't understand the world yet, but even at his tender age he sees that she's contradicting herself. How can they be alone, when they're stuck with all the others? All she can do is make up excuses for her husband, serve as his accomplice. She's never on the boy's side; she always supports her husband, who only takes the boy out on these trips so that he can carry the food and the Thermos of coffee, because his own hands won't stop shaking.

The boy thinks about this as he sits in the blind where they go every Sunday, where he gets bored as the hunters talk among themselves: about work, their cars, their in-laws. He hates the waiting, the off-colour jokes, the noise of the shots; he feels like an errand boy whose job is to run and fetch Thermos flasks and cigarettes. He'd prefer to go and play football with his friends on the grass at the edge of the estate, to spend his pocket money on table football players and watch the older boys show off their motorbikes and flirt with the neighbourhood girls. One day he'll have a bike, a big one, one of the bikes that deafens you as it drives past. All the boys will envy him, and all the girls will fight among themselves to be the one that he allows to ride with him in exchange for putting his hand up her dress and kissing her. He already knows what his helmet will look like, black with red stripes, so that when he drives through the suburbs, all the old people taking the air will cross themselves when they see a red line pass by.

But the worst part of it all for the kid is the undergrowth itself. Its insolent greenness overwhelms him, that single monotonous colour that stares at him from all sides, which changes its tones in an attempt to confuse him, which watches him, which lies in wait. He has never been able to accustom himself to this excess of colour. It reminds him of the television light that fills the living room every night, just before the fighting starts. Perhaps it is the tree trunks, so close to one another that they look like the palings of a fence, or else it might be the smell of dew on leaves, that sticks to the roof of his mouth and gives a mineral flavour to everything he tastes. It is the same taste as blood in the mouth, now that he comes to think of it.

It might be because of the eternal trembling in his father's hands, but every time he raises the rifle, it fires.

The boy might be scared of the pain that has suddenly hit his head, that makes him raise his hands to his temples. Did he start to feel the pain before or after the shot? The kid would swear that it was before he heard the shouts and everything started to go blurry.

The man waiting in the luxurious and impersonal hotel suite is nervous. He is waiting for something that is taking too long to arrive and so he is pacing the room. He is wearing a tailored suit that makes him look respectable without being ostentatious. He undoes his tie and starts to feel impatient. He has tried, but without success, to push away the migraine that bites at his head, the ghost of a childhood bullet.

He has not been able to relax at all: not by getting away from people, not by doing a line or two of coke. He calls his campaign director when the pain becomes as bad as sunburn.

'Hey ... Where has she got to? When did you tell her to come?' He hates being made to wait and his annoyance grows ever stronger, given the pain that he feels, at once so familiar and so unbearable.

There are a few soft knocks at the door.

'Oh, there she is. Leave it. I'll see you at breakfast tomorrow ... No worries.'

He puts the mobile in the inside pocket of his jacket. In spite of the pain, he opens the door with an automatic smile, a smile carved from the security that comes from private schools, country clubs and diaries filled with double-barrelled names. He has invested a worker's dull earnings into the perfect business card: the best possible dentistry.

'People vote for men with good teeth,' was the first thing his assessor said to him. 'Think about

Kennedy, or Reagan. The electorate, bless them, associates dental hygiene with moral integrity.'

It's funny that it is easier to have a perfect smile than to get rid of this damn steel finger that presses across his skull.

The hooker is waiting in the corridor. She is a young woman with copper-coloured hair and deep pools for eyes. Thank the Lord, she isn't too pale. He doesn't like the fizzy-aspirin shade that has become all the rage with women recently. He prefers a bit of colour in the cheeks; he prefers women not to look like invalids. He likes classy women, which means that he likes hookers to be hookers, but not to look like hookers. She is in an expensive overcoat, cinched at the waist, and high heels. She could be an executive or else a journalist, one of those who look after every single detail of their appearance in order to make the whole appear the result of genetics and carelessness. She is not carrying a bag. The security team will have confiscated it, to prevent any recording devices getting into the room.

'Come in. Don't just stand there in the hall.'

He invites her in with an almost condescending gesture, a jerk of the chin that one would use with almost anyone lower down on the invisible social scale; a clumsy attempt to overcome his own shyness.

She comes in, takes a couple of steps, makes herself at home. She looks at him with a smile that is so open it can only be fake. No hooker likes her job, and none of them would smile sincerely. He knows this because he often resorts to the services of escorts. He has spent months crisscrossing Spain on the electoral trail, miles and miles of shaking sweaty hands, meaningless meetings, cookie-cutter interviews, and flashbulbs going off in his face all the time. Sex with strangers is the only thing that relaxes him, and calms that implacable finger that is always stirring up his brains.

'They don't speak Spanish,' his campaign chief has assured him, and he is the man who sets up these meetings. 'It's better like this. You have to be sure that they can't understand what you say, and, most importantly, that they keep their mouths shut. If that's what you want.'

'Is it the same company as usual?'

'Calm down. You can trust them. I don't know how they do it, but they keep the women under control. They know how to put the squeeze on them, or their families.'

The man prefers not to think about these sordid things; it's not his problem: there are no shadows in his life. He pours himself a whisky with a lot of ice and sits down on the sofa. He starts to feel better after the first sip.

'Would you like a drink?'

If she has understood him, she does not bother to show that she has. Nor does she seem impressed by the luxury that surrounds them. He thinks that this is normal; nowadays no one is impressed by such conspicuous consumption. She must be from the east, from one of these Balkanised countries where people-trafficking is the only thing that adds numbers to the GDP.

'What's your name?' he asks, drawling the syllables as he speaks.

She's foreign, not a retard. Don't speak to her like she's an idiot.

The girl comes over to him and stops a hand's breadth away. She opens her overcoat and gets to her knees. She is not wearing anything underneath. Her nakedness does not clash with the décor of the room, and her gestures are not at all vulgar.

She puts her arms around him and he feels her fingers on his back, and the smell of her hair filling his senses. The colours around him seem to take on new shades and tones, become more defined, as though someone had adjusted the contrast on reality.

She slowly removes his clothes, and stands up. Her body is like that of an animal stretching into itself. He is intrigued by this strange woman, and lets her stroke his penis as he fondles her breasts.

Their skins become wet and moisture starts to flood their orifices. The woman opens her lower lips, inviting him to penetrate her; sweat mingles with her vaginal secretions, thickening them until they form a mother-of-pearl jelly that is viscous as amniotic fluid.

She laughs and begins to speak. Her words are like fingernails on a blackboard; they put his teeth on edge at the same time as they hypnotise him. She keeps on speaking, surely trying to excite him further. He lets himself go, his clumsy movements the same ones he learnt in the neon roadside brothels of his youth, but she leads him on with the deftness of a nurse. His swollen glans is the head of a semi-developed foetus, looking to make its way back into the womb, the nest where it was formed and where it feels at home, the familiar uterine darkness welcoming him once again.

For him, light has always been something foreign and treacherous, a phenomenon that defines shapes and forms, makes them angular and sharp. Reality becomes a dangerous place; objects become concrete and acquire strange and malignant capabilities. On the other hand, in the dark everything is uncertain and evil only exists in potential, without being fully defined. Forms disappear, sharp edges are smoothed, and all things recover their neonatal state, in which no such thing as a threat exists. That is why he closes his eyes and imagines himself sinking into a shrouded lake, protected by the fluids that pour from the young woman.

She sticks her tongue out and licks his chin. He feels as though she has recognised his soul in all its darkness and patches of light, because it is easy for words to falsify reality, but the skin never lies. Pores give access to secretions which tell her about desire, those pheromones dissolved in mineral salts, the sweat that smells of being in heat, of fear of ridicule, of pretensions to power.

She lines up the entrance to her vagina for him to penetrate her. He is in a hurry to submerge himself in the protected zone that is her sex: an endangered species looking for its sanctuary. The dampness wraps around him; it is his ally and confirms that they are both equally excited.

She licks her lips. He interprets this gesture as a provocation and pulls her hair back until her chin lifts. She laughs as she feels his attack and murmurs a little song in a language he does not understand, no doubt a lewd little ditty from the miserable hole where she was born. She raises her voice and he feels even more aroused as he imagines the filthy fantasies that she is singing him.

Inside her is warm and viscous. He does not feel any end to it, and this surprises him. Normally, when he pushes himself inside a woman, he feels his penis touching the neck of the womb, but in this case he feels nothing.

This vagina is an abyss, a bottomless mine dug into her flesh.

He carries on thrusting, with an appetite aroused by the song she sings. He thinks about giving her a slap and telling her to shut up, but he thinks she wouldn't understand and that she's probably used to being knocked around anyway.

These pre-orgasmic thoughts electrify him and bring him into a state that borders on sensory effervescence. But the space inside her, rather than exciting him further, makes him worried: it's not normal to find this kind of disproportion in a thin woman; there is no voluptuousness to this body, certainly not enough to justify such a cavernous vagina.

Something isn't right. He gets worried and hits her. It's a full-on slap, a loud backhander, like a hefty electoral promise. The young woman's face does not change; she is still fixed on some point far distant from the person who is manhandling her.

She carries on singing in that language which now sounds to him like the scraping of a hundred cicadas, forcing its way into the twists and folds of his brain in order to take possession of him. Once the hellish noise is plunging at him, panic comes quickly, attracted by the irregularities in his body's movements, in his co-copulator's flesh.

Her face is now a moving canvas; her eyes have moved to the side and her mouth is larger. Her nose and ears have almost disappeared and the man thinks that she looks like an eel, but also like his mother, when he looked at her from the door to her room, thrown down on her bed, her back naked. It is a grimace that could be a cynical smirk or a rictus of pain, depending on the angle.

She is now no longer next to him, but looking at him from the end of the room. The lights and the sounds die away and time fades to nothing. He can make out her figure against the furthest window and although he wants to stand up, he finds he is unable to. His limbs are frozen and do not respond to his commands, although he can feel how his guts expand as he lies there. He wants to ask her what's happening, what the fuck she put into his drink to make him hallucinate in four dimensions, but it's impossible for him to move his head and she has moved out of his field of vision. He can't see her and he wants to call her. The words that fall out of his mouth are different, and have nothing to do with his intentions. He listens to himself, and cannot stop himself from retching.

Your clothes do not look like that Samarra cloth you once wore, Vanth. The walls around you are the same white as the stars that hurt your eyes when you look at them, searching for reasons why men dress their habitations in such anti-natural colours. Were the walls of Ur not the colour of golden wheatfields? This can only be the work of madmen with no culture, abandoned creatures with traditions of paper, for these walls say nothing of the men who have lived here before, they tell the story of no family, they say nothing of the rites that have been here professed, or of the way in which these people buried their dead. They are naked walls of houses piled one atop the other, like the cemetery holes in Agra, or the grain silos in the Menfe gate on the banks of the Nile ... There is no silence here, for men are now frightened by the absence of noise, and we need constant stimulation in order to feel alive.

What is he talking about? And why is his belly swelling in this way? Why is his mind being filled with the memories of thousands of lives? As if nailed to the ground, he feels the blood loop lazily in his veins and his abdomen stretch, little by little: a globe of skin forming without him being able to do anything about it. 'It must be the drugs,' he says to himself, and tries to relax and allow the sensations to dissipate somewhere, somehow. He cannot close his eyes, and the ceiling becomes high as a cathedral: it moves away, or rather he sinks into some gaseous plane. The floor is an elastic mesh that pulls him down, before releasing him to fly into the heavens.

The bed you are accustomed to lie on is not as hard as the mats in the temple of Marduk, the ones where you awoke for the first time; neither are they as uncomfortable as the straw mattresses of the Cihuacalli, where you slept before you became free. You offer your body in the least of all the canopied beds, ever since you realised that you no longer needed the protection of the priests. Perhaps it is safer to march under their banner, to avoid the ridicule of the Pharisees and the blows of the pimps, but blows cannot harm your skin, and neither can poisonous words. I am going to fall apart now, like the wet cardboard where your poison falls, like the glass that breaks under your strength; I will fall apart quickly, although it will seem to me an eternity. I will send news of my own death to whoever wishes to hear it. Will there be anyone on the other side?

He tries to avoid thinking about the presence in the room with him. She is still there; he can feel her in the vibrations of the floor, walking in circles round his room, although he cannot see her. He sinks down further and further, while his belly keeps growing. Perhaps it is she who controls the web that imprisons him. When he starts to feel some force moving him upwards, his back gently arches, but in some region of his brain he realises he is immobile, and that none of this is really happening.

But now he is used to the darkness and finds that the woman is walking in elliptic orbits around him, her eyes shining and lacquered, visible even in the shadows. He can only see her when she walks in front of him, but he would swear that her auburn hair has disappeared. She is not singing now, except if he listens extremely hard. He has not stopped talking, and there is still a knot of nausea in his throat.

When I called my campaign manager to get him to discreetly organise me an escort to spend the night with, I didn't think I'd end up speaking Aramaic. I, who can speak in all the languages of the Peninsula, am chanting psalms in a dead tongue. Zer moduz, Vanth? De quin aster et vas despenjar? Cantos infestaches antes ca min? I told you I was a polyglot and you did not believe me, nor do you recall my photograph that covers the walls and lampposts of the city. You too attracted many walking hard-ons with those shoes you wore, the boots with 'follow me' written on their soles. They followed you and you set them free. Would you do that with me? You open your mouth, I know not if it is to swallow me once and for all or laugh at me, now that I am no more than a puppet, rotten on the inside.

His stomach is now as big as that of a pregnant woman nearing her term, and the rest of him begins to swell: his hands, his legs, his feet, his genitals. All his limbs grow like ripening fruit and he keeps on talking without stopping, forced up into one of the lower levels of the stratosphere.

The woman walks in a circle round him without pause, constantly licking her lips and sucking her fingers. The man does not know which is worse: the spasms that have colonised his digestive system, the paralysis that incapacitates him, or the movements of this woman with a face like a deep-sea creature who is walking like some predatory beast. The darkness around them takes on an unbearable greenish sheen.

I stand in death's waiting room, at some point in time that will only last a second or two, but which will expand in my mind to free me up to speak for hours. I am a photonaut, travelling this black-and-white tunnel in search of the brilliant light that I can only see at a distance. Every dying man sees this same damn light, but no one knows what it really is. They wonder about it, think that it might be the other side, paradise, limbo, the passageway to another dimension, the entrance to The Beyond. Now I understand that it is no more than a star, that this is what we see when we die: we become once again the plasma of which we are a part. Life is a twisting journey in which we change state to return to our primal structures. This is the same as going home; this is fusion with the nucleus of whatever once gave life to the molecules that now animate us.

The man is turning into a sphere of grease, fluids and keratin. He wonders what the elastic capacity of human skin might be, if it can burst in the same way that it can inflate. Now he no longer feels that he is pushing upwards. He is floating. He is in a fragile state that might change at any moment; he could easily fall back into the web which holds him and which he is starting to believe he will never escape. 'I am dreaming awake,' he lies to himself. The migraine has sunk its roots into his head and has grown fat in his body; all he has to do now is wait for it to flower. The female presence in the room has turned into his satellite, always showing him the same face.

What did you do to me? Did you castrate me like you did the Scythians who raped you in the southern Ural steppe, or like you did the Hirpini who tried to take advantage of your body in the mountains of Lucania, or like you did the Geats who pursued you through the Västergötland fjords? Now I know that you called them to you with your hips and your secretions, that you made desire flame up in their crotches and that they let themselves be called to you without suspecting a thing. I also understand that there are sexual practices that are so complex they require days of preparation; that you can keep a man at the brim of ejaculation for hours at a time, until he is driven mad; that you can make a woman experience dozens of orgasms in an hour—so many that her heart stops.

The woman has stopped walking and has approached the man. In spite of the darkness, he can see every single detail of her teleplastic face: her eyes that have shifted to the side of her head; the irises that have opened wide into two stagnant pools. He cannot see the ears or the nose; it is as though they had never existed, and the head has grown larger and pushed the face forwards. She sits down next to the man and lays her hands on the belly that stretches free of the swollen body.

He sees a pair of bony hands with long phalanges, tipped with claws, stroking him like a prize. The jaws open and reveal toothless gums. Several prehensile tongues reach out and stroke his face, and he feels their rough surface stroking his cheeks.

I don't see my life flashing before my eyes. They lied to us. All I see before me is your life and your couplings; I smell the sweat in the shirts that embrace you, I feel the salty, burning semen that has bathed you over the centuries.

You have left a trail behind you, of glassy eyes and purple tongues, bleeding gums and torn fingernails, swollen labia and orphaned penises. The people who thought that you were their victim realised that they were the prey and the people who thought they would deflower you only had time to see how their shadows faded against the wall. You never leave witnesses.

Black milk flows from the woman's breasts. The man starts to wonder if this trance will have any after-effects, because so much trauma has to be real on some level. He needs to move, to change his posture, but his body will not respond. His limbs are grotesque versions of themselves, muscles bent to the limit of what their cells can cope with. She is there, next to him, and the globe of his belly lies before him, and he is followed by the words that come out of his mouth and the damn headache. He cannot bear the greenish tint that the darkness has taken on.

I wonder if I am redeemed, if this is the object of this ritual. I forgive all those who thought that you were a monster of this world, Vanth. They did not know that you are not of this world. Your infertility is our salvation, because you cannot sow our house with demons. I do not want to know what would happen if you could bear others like you; how many more victims would be added to those who have already been initiated into your mysteries. Is there a cult of your work and offices? Now

I see that your eyes are not black but rather reflective; they show us the darkness in our souls. Your skin, by contrast, is transparent. My eyes can follow the flow of blood through even the finest capillaries; each particular fluid with its own path, bringing life to this body that is trained to bring pleasure and to destroy.

The woman holds the swollen man with the tenderness of a mother beast cradling her pup. This is no hallucination: his body has attained truly grotesque dimensions. His head hurts from having so much green darkness around him; perhaps it never stopped hurting. Now he understands the anticipatory value of pain, the same that he felt when the bullet came into him, years ago. He must have understood that something horrible was about to happen, but he preferred to ignore the signs. Prostrate and defenceless, with an eel-woman by his side weeping milk from her breasts, he wants to cry out from pain and fear, or even from fear alone, but he cannot. The words he is saying will not let him cry out; this speech that he had not prepared for his campaign has taken control of his body. He tries to make his throat close, but his vocal cords have been taken control of by this woman who looks at him with hungry eyes.

Who were your parents? I am sorry for asking such intimate questions, but I feel like I have known you forever. I know almost your entire life. Isn't pain the best way to bring spirits together? Love is overrated; I know that now. Suffering is a truer sentiment, because it is not carried away by any flighty affection, but rather remains anchored in the sensations registered in the flesh, which has more memory than a million servants. Now I know all the lives that you cut short, all those whom you locked away in iron fetters, embalmed in their own fats, whose torments and miseries you dried and preserved so that someone might try to decipher them when they dug them up, might try to identify them and study them, trying to understand their way of life, as though there were anything more to life than eating and fucking. But no one asks about you or your family. Do you have a family? I cannot see back any further than the first time you opened your eyes on this planet, I don't know which other worlds you visited before this one, before ours. Do creatures in other galaxies copulate in the same way? Did you find equal pleasure in killing them just after the moment of orgasm, or did you search for more sophisticated ways of bringing their lives to an end? Don't look at me with that smile on your face; you must have come from someone's belly, even if it was the belly of a creature that does not approximate to any human knowledge.

They are knocking at the door. The woman opens her mouth so wide that her jaws become dislocated, her chest sinks back and her head strikes forward as though she were shrieking, but she makes no noise.

The man shudders at this silent cry. He feels dizzy, and senses that his cheeks are also inflating.

He wants his head to explode once and for all, just to stop himself from speaking, and to stop the migraine from torturing him. Voices outside the room call his name, but he cannot answer them.

The woman reaches over with her sea-creature head to kiss him and he feels her lips like the mouth of a remora catching on with no intention of letting him go. His words can no longer be heard in the room, although his throat carries on producing them. He can't breathe; the pain in his head clouds all his thoughts. He tries to breathe through his nose, but the swelling of his facial cartilage means that no air can reach him. His consciousness starts to fade, his spleen shuts down, his guts, his kidneys and his pancreas, his lungs, and last of all his heart and brain. The last thing he sees is the image of the woman leaning over him, and dissolving into thousands of green sparks.

The void will swallow me, although this instant will never entirely arrive. I am trapped in the moments that precede death; I am the astronaut poised forever at event horizon, close enough to see my end a matter of inches away, able to imagine the effect of massive gravity, but too far away still to be swallowed by the black hole. I can envision my end, but the actual denouement is always distant from me; this is the nature of my punishment. At least I won't end up like that hysterical nun who wanted to take advantage of your openness to force you into lesbian servitude. She stayed rolled up in her own tongue, which you stretched out as though it were an infinite piece of chewing-gum, so she could die forever suffocated in her slow agony. Neither will I end up like that train of Berbers who tried to profane your nooks and crannies, all of them forced for hours, under the baking Maghreb sun, to suffer the desires of their camels. I will die for centuries, centuries which will turn into aeons, which will in their turn transform into dust motes in some constellation. I should have paid attention to the signs, but I chose to ignore them. How did they taste, my words?

There is a swollen body lying at the foot of the sofa. Judging from the genitals, it is a male. Its eyes are open and roll backwards so just the whites are showing.

I understand that my function is to feed you, and now that you are sated, you can continue to make use of this Earth. You are what you are, and that is your nature; and no one can ask pardon for being what they are. You have hunted murderers and rapists, martyrs and outstanding men, women possessed by demons, old women, saints and infants. Good and evil are concepts that mean nothing to your race, that do not contribute anything or add any value. Perhaps we will see each other in some fresh place, but I imagine that all your first meetings are also final ones. I know that it was nothing personal, that it is not the moral hide in which your prey cloaks itself that interests you, but rather opportunism.

'It's like he was trying to look inside himself,' the first forensic officer says as he comes onto the crime scene.

'What could have caused this?' his colleague asks.

'What, or who?' the first one replies, pointing at the woman's overcoat and the high heels which are ready to be bagged as evidence.

INCHWORM

'Something like "Ashes to Ashes" wouldn't have happened if it hadn't have been for "Inchworm". There's a child's nursery rhyme element in it, and there's something so sad and mournful and poignant about it. It kept bringing me back to the feelings of those pure thoughts of sadness that you have as a child, and how they're so identifiable even when you're an adult.'

David Bowie, interview in *Performing Songwriter*, 2003

THE MOTHER, A GLOBULAR SHIP. UMBILICAL CORDS that provide food, remove waste, hydrate, keep warm, and monitor. A child safe at the centre of an

Author's Note: The video of the song 'Ashes to Ashes' has remained with me ever since I saw it for the first time aged eight. I was both fascinated and scared by it. There is an image that appears twice in the video (at 2.17 and 3.23): the image of Bowie hanging from a wall, in a kind of life support system, with a number of tubes emerging from his suit. When I read up on the song, I found that Bowie had used elements from a song by Danny Kaye in the film *Hans Christian Andersen* (1952), one of his favourite films. This story is an exploration of my obsession with Bowie's song.

45

ectopic pregnancy, passenger in an unnatural womb made from exotic fibres, travelling through the guts of the universe at a speed hypothesised by scientists without money to investigate, and who substitute their lack of funds for imagination.

He is hanging from a wall that could be the floor, or the roof, for there is no up or down here, no left or right, no centre or periphery. Zero gravity is a blanket that wraps round him, a familiar and calming sensation that keeps his brain afloat. He feels fluids entering and leaving his body, he hears a noise, like that of water boiling, and remembers some English china cups, with hand-painted roses and gold rims, on a tablecloth decorated in brown and orange flowers. It is cold outside, and raining, but inside it is warm and welcoming, and Peggy takes the kettle off the fire and pours the steaming liquid into the cups. There is a plate of gingerbread, and as his mother pours the milk, he takes a piece and nibbles it in the hope that the tea will soon get cool enough to drink. There is an older brother and a father somewhere, but not in this memory.

The ship takes care of him, brings him the nutrition he requires, makes the relevant adjustments to his body. He feels expansions and contractions, but cannot sense where in his body they are taking place. Right now he would happily sit and take a cup of tea in the Bromley kitchen. If he makes the effort, he can taste the gingerbread in his mouth, the flavour he likes so much. There's no need to make the effort, though, because shortly after thinking of it, he feels the taste of ginger scratchy on his tongue. He licks his lips.

'Thank you, Peggy.'

He still cannot bring himself to say 'mother'.

Every time he thinks of Houston he wants to laugh and the walls laugh with him, carrying the echo of his guffaw in all directions. How much those bastards must be wishing he were retransmitting everything he saw! Control must have given him up for dead and would be writing their report about him: 'died on active service'. But he is alive, feeling better than ever, and can laugh at them from his privileged womb.

He had opened up the porthole and launched himself to the stars. You have to have balls to do that.

He would never have died on livestream, as Houston wanted, sending out his final moments to all the televisions on the planet and breaking all viewing records. 'If anything goes wrong,' they said, 'keep in the centre of the image so that we can record you.' This is entirely scientific, they never stopped saying, but the rocket was filled with products that he had to show to the camera at precisely agreed times: the Miami Gators shirt at the instant he entered nominal programmed orbit; Landa soft drinks at least three times a day; the Cosmos watch every time Houston entered into conversation with him; the AirAmericana baseball cap when the launch manoeuvres had been completed. He would bet anything you like that they would have used his death to sell insurance policies, cars, or some ersatz champagne with a Frenchified name. He imagines the Defence Department attaché rubbing his hands at this new national drama, and the GNN executives, the ones with the exclusive broadcast rights, working out what they were going to earn in advertising revenue.

He's screwed up their plans, but he feels no regret. The one who is travelling through the guts of space, a long way from Bromley, is him. The Houston crowd, with all their attachés, executives, directors, doctors and engineers, are all back home, some of them cuddling up to their wives, some of them fighting with them, and the rest ignoring them.

He is not sure—he can't be—but he thinks that he will never see Marianne again. It is one of those certainties that he has gathered over the course of his life, the kind you feel rather than think; like the sun rising in the east and setting in the west. Marianne and the bend of her naked back when he stroked her in bed. Marianne trying on clothes and looking at herself in the mirror without knowing which outfit to pick. Marianne smoking at the window, dressed in an old shirt, the rain licking the panes behind her.

Here you can't hear anything, like in a sound-proofed recording studio, but he doesn't know why he thinks of things like that; he's never been in a recording studio in his life.

He is an accidental astronaut, a British pilot who was working on supersonic planes, more for fun than out of a sense of vocation, but who was tempted by a trip over the Atlantic. One of those who was seduced by the clouds in America, which are much whiter, like American teeth; and the sky is bluer and the cars are bigger, like the egos of the people driving them. A signature on a contract, and he could start earning dollars and debt, to buy a prefab life and escape from a frozen version of England.

The silence is so deep that it seems to squeak. He hears his blood travelling through every single one of the capillaries that crisscross his body, and he thinks of the noise made by the engines of the planes he used to fly, back when he did not have tubes entering his face. He laughs again and the whole ship imitates him.

The ship's laughter is deep, cavernous, not as metallic as he might have expected from a structure that travels through space. He realises that this is not a rocket like the one he launched in a few days ago. Perhaps it is not a ship as people on Earth might understand it, and his hair stands on end as he thinks this, but something must take place in his circulatory system, because fear has no time to set itself up in him; rather, a welcoming calm wraps round every one of his cells. Whatever they're giving him is powerful and effective.

He doesn't even react when an image of the pilots from the previous mission, Murphy and Connor, stock still with glassy eyes, appears before him like a Polaroid, the mossy colours eating at their silhouettes, using up the oxygen so quickly that they did not even have the chance to put their suits on. This image, sent to the press by someone at Houston, and used for the covers of newspapers and magazines, created a movement aimed at raising money to send a mission to get their bodies back. Lots of brands signed up to it.

They said to him: 'Jones, we have a mission for you. It's so simple that you'll be back before you know you've left. We need to get the bodies of Murphy and Connor back, and also we're going to take the chance to put a satellite in orbit. You'll be famous. A hero. Generations to come will remember you admiringly. They'll name streets and squares after you, maybe even an airport. Children will want to be like you, and parents will use you as an example.'

The pay was high and the risks were low. They had discovered how the fire in the oxygen tank had started; they explained this hundreds of times. He had nothing to fear, they assured him, although the mission was being put together hastily, to take advantage of the public mood.

It all happened fast, too fast.

The valves on the oxygen tank failed again.

The ship reacts, anticipating his needs and repairing him, stabilising him, optimising him. There is a lot of work still to do, he knows, because he lost consciousness and probably a number of other things when the oxygen in his suit ran out, the alarms from the sensors beating at his ears. He saw the rocket up against the space station, Murphy's and Connor's sarcophagus, a bright point in the distance with the Earth as a backdrop. They were orbiting above the Pacific Ocean. He knew that he was starting to feel drowsy, and that he would never awake from his dark dream, and so he turned round and set off in the opposite direction from the planet. And so he remained asleep, wrapped in the millions of twinkling lights that watched him from every angle, an impressive blanket of stars.

He can't recall how long he has been in this state.

The next thing he remembers is a room with walls so white they seem unreal. Mountain peaks in travel brochures are not this colour, neither are clouds this clean when they hang over the desert. He is not wearing his helmet, but is unsure whether he is still wearing the spacesuit. He hurts from head to toe.

The sense of hanging somewhere, even before he opens his eyes and sees the tubes connected to his body, is the next thing he perceives.

He is Jonah in the belly of the whale, and is immobilised: the ship is looking after him. He does not need to ask for anything, because as soon as he even thinks of it, it arrives. And the pain goes away.

He thinks about his brother. What was his name? Larry ... Perry ... Terry! He was called Terry, and the strains of Little Richard reverberate in this space that he occupies along with his tubes, and which could be a hall, a room, a corridor, a theatre or all of them at the same time.

Just as he knows he will never see Marianne again, he is also sure that Terry will appear at any moment, with a record player under one arm and several Miles Davis albums on vinyl. Yes, he would not be surprised to see him here at all, in spite of the fact that he has been dead for several months.

Terry had the balls to jump.

Good old Terry, who took him to gigs and gave him cigarettes behind his mother's back. The same guy whose father despised him, because he was the son of a former boyfriend of his mother's, and whose grandmother mistreated him because of the shame he had brought upon the family. It is only madness that treated him well.

Terry would have liked to have seen the launch from Cape Canaveral, and would have been tickled pink to see the images of his opening the airlock and heading out, leaving the capsule empty and depressurised.

He would have been the only one to applaud.

He would have been the only one to understand it.

He wishes that he were there, with him. Speaking about girls and jazz and the bands that had recently formed in the neighbourhood.

'Can Peggy hear us?'

Here he is. Sitting in one of the armchairs in the living room, his head pushed back and smoking as though this were the only cigarette left in the universe. The record player is on his knees: Fats Domino.

'Peggy is everywhere,' he replies to his brother. 'We are inside her.'

Terry looks at him after a long drag on his cigarette.

'At least your old man doesn't hang around here. Or the witch, or granny. Jesus, I hate them so much ... Hey, kid, what happened to you? You look terrible.'

'I'm happy to see you, Terry. You can't know how happy I am.'

His brother carries on smoking in silence. And now it's 'Tutti Frutti' by Little Richard, furious. The walls dance and make a sound like a dozen pressure cookers letting off steam.

'You jumped, man.'

'I jumped. Did you see it?'

'If you'd seen what they looked like back at Control! Everyone in Houston had their mouth open. I've never heard anyone swear at you so thoroughly.'

When Terry laughs, it's like going back to Bromley, knowing that there is tea waiting for you in the kitchen.

'I was already damned.'

Terry answers before he disappears.

'You never were.'

It's funny: 'getting high' has stopped being a metaphor. He guesses he's hallucinating under the effects of whatever they're giving him. The ship? Peggy?

Is there anyone there?

Aside from Terry, he hasn't seen anyone else, no red-haired aliens, no crazy doctors, not a single sad clown. He feels certain membranes regenerating, organs which stop needing outside assistance and which start to function independently again, and he thinks that he was not prepared for what came after the jump. You jump, throw yourself into the void; you put the gun to your temple, the noose round your neck; you open the gas tap, leap into the water, and you already know what is going to happen. But you're not ready for what happens afterwards, because there is no concept of an *afterwards* in your mind.

He doesn't know where to go.

He doesn't know who or what picked him up.

He can't understand that Terry has left him.

He feels insignificant and tiny, like a worm in a metallic flower from some infinite garden. The first man to reach Kuiper's Belt, maybe even the first to enter the Oort Cloud, and who is now going to enter zones that scientists have only imagined. He also knows that the vessel has kept in constant movement, and that it is moving away from the Sun, although he does not know how he knows. Peggy had made him understand it somehow, implanting the thoughts into his brain in the same way that she has put substances into him to restore his cells.

It all smacks a bit of magic.

He is an astronaut hanging from a wall, in an omniscient vessel moving away from the Sun.

It is a vessel, a cosmic creature, an anomaly in space-time, a hallucination of a junkie rock star, a music video of a mime in a Pierrot costume, the dream of an old man with a bandaged face and two buttons for eyes, the mental flight of a child being raped by his father's best friend in the kitchen in Bromley, who dreams he is an astronaut hanging from a wall, in a ship moving away from the Sun.

> *Two and two are four;*
> *Four and four are eight;*
> *Eight and eight are sixteen;*
> *Sixteen and sixteen are thirty-two.*

Inchworm, inchworm,
measuring the marigolds,
you and your arithmetic,
you'll probably go far.

Inchworm, inchworm,
measuring the marigolds,

seems to me you'd stop and see
how beautiful they are.

Seems to me you'd stop and see
how beautiful they are.
Seems to me you'd stop and see
how beautiful they are ...

ALICE

ALICE WOKE UP AND REMEMBERED ONLY HER NAME. It was a strange feeling not to recall anything from her past but only to know two things: her name and that she had been subjected to the treatment.

She accessed the authorised facts of her new custom-made identity thanks to a touch panel located on top of the bedcovers, right at her fingertips, and learned that she was thirty-five, single and good with plants.

The room in Dr Joy's Clinic was barren, like Alice's past. Even though everything seemed designed to soothe the patient who passed through it, the whiteness was overwhelming. The only hints of colour were the projected pastel holograms on the walls, inviting the clients to relax and seek assistance in case of anxiety.

Apart from the bed where she lay, there was a round table with two chairs and a cupboard.

No windows or doors were visible. The panel did not offer additional information and no other connecting devices were visible. She wanted to call a nurse but didn't know how. As soon as she began to sit up, the bed adopted an upright position, and a woman in a white coat materialised from someplace at the back of the room.

'Don't stand up just yet, dear. You need to rest. It's normal to feel a bit confused and dizzy. A full night's sleep will help you regain your strength, and tomorrow morning you will be discharged.'

'So, I paid for a full treatment? I must have been pretty damn rich!'

'I can't tell you, sweetie, even if I knew. You see, I'm a post-service nurse. All the preparations were done through our pre-treatment process to ensure absolute confidentiality. Nobody from this facility holds any information about your past and—according to the terms of your contract—you were transferred to a different city to minimise any accidental revelations. Nobody knows you here, darling!'

Alice did not feel particularly reassured. If anything, she was even more confused, even if her left earlobe was greatly swollen, a clear indication of her high level of happiness. The earlobe of the nurse was even more engorged—the size of a walnut—and Alice asked herself if the woman was genuinely cheerful or if her high spirits were artificially induced.

'What am I supposed to do now? Are there any instructions left by my *prior me*?'

'Of course! Just a few, but we'll talk about it tomorrow, honey. Now you need to relax. Drugs have been stored in your system during therapy to be released around this time and give you a good night's sleep.'

The next time Alice opened her eyes the nurse was already there, with the same joyful expression, her earlobe even more engorged.

'Did you have a pleasant sleep? Are you feeling rested enough? You look gorgeous this morning! It is quite late though, so we have to hurry up with the last formalities before you're discharged.'

Alice felt refreshed but more confused than the previous day. She felt surprised by the nurse's excessive diligence, her plastic smile, and the fact that she did not remember getting dressed.

'Who dressed me? I don't remember putting any clothes on.'

'I did it myself, sweetie. Don't worry. Aren't all us girls built the same? I was very careful not to wake you up. Cameron helped me, of course.'

'Who is Cameron?'

The nurse chose not to answer. Instead, she continued to stand in front of the bed, in the exact same spot where Alice remembered her from the day before.

'I wish I could spend the whole day talking to you, chatting about girl stuff and so on. But, you see, time is marching on and we are a bit behind schedule. You need to sign the discharge form, and this other one too, which is the receipt for your belongings. But remember that you are Alice C., so make sure that your signature reflects your new identity. This envelope contains your new ID, your medical records as relocated into your new registered legal persona, and the address of your new home. I hear it's a lovely place!'

Alice found that she was already wearing shoes and had the strap of a white travel bag over her shoulder. She was starting to resent the absence of colour and the nurse's sympathetic tone.

'Dr Joy's Clinic assures you that all the instructions specified in your contract have been followed. You'll have a job, in accordance with your abilities, which will pay for your room and board at the address I gave you. No further information will be provided in order to avoid any interference with your new life. You'll be extremely happy! We hope our service was to your liking, and that you'll recommend us to your future acquaintances.'

'Wait a minute! You can't just throw me out like that. I have many questions ... my *prior me* must have known that I'd be needing more to work with.'

The nurse's smile widened.

'Do you really remember nothing from your past, Miss C.?'

'The only thing I'm sure about is my name!'

'Excellent!' The nurse clapped her hands, as if Alice's confusion delighted her. 'That means we did our job properly.'

'Didn't you hear me? I *demand* answers. I must have arranged for something more. Just to understand this situation.'

The face in front of her did not reveal any signs of annoyance.

'Decisions were taken in advance by your prior personality, who instructed us not to disclose *anything* else. Nobody knew you better than yourself. Honey, I guess you have to show a bit of faith in your previous *you*. You have the chance to start your life from scratch. What a wonderful opportunity! Embrace it!'

And Alice was out. Her travel bag followed her like a white shadow; she didn't even know what was in it. The clinic was brand new and generic, the type of construction that could contain anything from a laboratory to a high-tech venture company or a block of trendy lofts. There was no indication of a clinic operating inside: no sign, no logo, not even a name on an intercom.

The whole thing looked very suspicious to Alice, who was still confused but strangely content. She touched her left earlobe and found it only a bit smaller than the day before. As she walked, she could feel the envelope that the nurse had given her. The envelope filled with enough strands of information to pursue a life.

Alice could remember general information with no problem—celebrity gossip, political and economic news up to around a month ago, lessons from school—but everything about her past was pitch black. There wasn't a CV in the envelope, or any prospect of finding out more. 'Good with plants' wasn't much to start with, but she assumed that either it was her hobby or she was inclined towards gardening because of her prior professional career. Having no family and no friends was also unsettling: was she asocial? Why had she taken such extreme measures to cut herself off from her past? She had to start trusting this new, unfamiliar person: herself. A leap of faith.

She must have had important reasons to buy the treatment, and a lot of cash. People sought personality cleaning services all the time to erase addictions, bad memories of cheating lovers or traumatic experiences, but an integral therapy was almost unheard of, and obscenely expensive. She wondered how she had had access to that amount of money, and what was so terrible or unbearable in her past life that she wanted to erase it so thoroughly.

She *wasn't* unhappy, but neither did she sense any elation. Maybe she could extract more information from the manager in the clinic, even try to talk to whoever was responsible for her surgery, or the salesperson in charge of her dossier.

She realised she had not paid attention to the name of the street when coming out of the clinic. She had been walking for a while and she could not find her way back. The city was unfamiliar: without an address, she could not ask for directions. The Data Sea could help her access some information and eventually find the location of the clinic; but without any Sea Board to connect with, that was out of the question. She sighed.

The envelope waited patiently in her hand. She opened it to access her Citizen Identification Print, the document that proved she was registered as a citizen in different Administrations. Her medical records—applied to her new identity—were included in the form of a data shell. There was a business card for a place called Groove Hills with an address, a telephone number and a name written in ink on the back: Mr Ellison, General Director.

There was no money in the envelope, or in the pockets of her trench coat, or in her jeans. She did not want to open the travel bag in the middle of the street, although something told her that there wasn't any money inside either. But she did check, and confirmed that there was no money or Board to hook to the Data Sea.

She asked a cleaning mech about the address on the card. The bulky machine pointed towards a park a dozen blocks away before resuming its vacuum assault on the pavement. Alice thought the cleaning was pointless, since she was the only person walking in the street. People took pods to reach their destinations, so strolling was regarded as almost unnatural.

'Why do you clean? Nobody's walking on the pavement.'

'I'm doing my job, ma'am.'

City-upkeep mechs were the only creatures other than her on the ground; the air was busy with pods of all shapes and sizes. The mech had spoken to her with the same politeness as the nurse.

'Forgive me. I just went through an integral personality cleaning treatment, and the drugs they gave me to control my anxiety seem to have worn off. Look at my earlobe: see what I mean?'

Alice tilted her head to show the mech her ear. The machine looked at it respectfully before resuming its work. Alice observed it almost with envy. The mech had a purpose in life: it knew its origins and, once its systems failed, would know its destiny.

'I guess I just need to talk to someone, and you've been so nice giving me directions ...'

'Do you require further assistance, ma'am?'

'I suppose you can call it that. I want a friendly face to listen to me, that's all.'

'I must call to your attention the fact that I do not possess a face, friendly or otherwise, ma'am. Therefore I do not qualify for the task.'

'It's just an expression. Aren't you familiar with human rhetoric? I bet you can listen. I *want* you to listen ... please.'

'I must comply with your orders, ma'am. Petitions are unnecessary.'

Alice pointed to the steps of a chic office building nobody climbed up anymore. Pod ports installed in the roof had relocated entrance halls to the higher ground. She took a seat.

'I would like you to sit next to me. Since I can't talk to myself, since I've only known *me* for a few hours, I guess talking to you will help me sort out my thoughts.'

'I can't sit, ma'am. I do not possess any articulations that would allow me to perform such an action.'

The mech was a medium height, yellow cylinder, with articulated arms and an anti-gravity booster that allowed it to float. Its body hid different tools, which the arms used to scrub, rinse, dry and suck.

'Just come closer, will you?'

'Ma'am, yes, ma'am.'

The machine hovered a few feet from Alice, facing her and waiting.

'An integral PCT! What was I thinking? You know how expensive the treatment is? I only know about one guy, an actor, who went through it, after his family died in a car accident while he was driving the car drunk. They said it costs as much as outfitting an interstellar pod. I must have been filthy rich.'

'I'm just a cleaner, ma'am. An android would be more suited for this assignment.'

Alice saw the rainbow blister in the machine's chassis. It was connected to the Data Sea, like the rest of the city-upkeep mechs.

'I don't want to deal with one of those pretentious human wannabes. Surely you can link to a sub-routine at the City Hall mainframe. Just connect me. You'll be my terminal.'

The mech hummed, the sound of a distant hive.

'I'm in, ma'am. Your earlier asseveration about being rich is a very logical explanation. However, it is not the only one. Do you want me to run a program with all the possible scenarios?'

'I know what you mean. There are different possibilities.'

'Well, ma'am, apart from being extremely wealthy yourself, you could also have been given the money by a donor, anonymously or not. Another scenario that accounts for it is that the treatment might not have been administered willingly but forcibly by a third party, again anonymously or not. There are multiple scenarios in any of those cases. I could build an algorithm to calculate possibilities also, taking into account all possible combinations of circumstances.'

'That won't be necessary. I get it.'

Alice looked up at the sky and saw only the heavy traffic. High lanes were filled with pods of all kinds, from personal to cargo. The city was displaying its veins, like a dissected body in a morgue.

'Did they give you a name at the factory?'

'Ma'am, I'm a city-upkeep mech, compact model 3000073.'

Alice let her gaze wander around until a flash commercial for a Sea Channel exclusively dedicated to eugenics caught her eye. It was displayed on every billboard screen at the same time.

'Can I call you Eugene? I think the name suits you. Do you like it, Eugene?'

'I do not possess a proper name, ma'am.'

The woman looked at the machine.

'I just gave you one; therefore, you have it. You must answer when I refer to you as Eugene.'

'Ma'am, yes, ma'am.'

'It's easier to converse with someone with a name. What do you think about the whole thing, Eugene? I need an external opinion and yours seems to me the only one around.'

'Well, ma'am, an integral personality cleaning therapy is one of the most complete services a person can undergo, but if the intention was a radical change, according to the algorithm, the probabilities of a gender reassignment grow almost exponentially.'

The woman stared back at the mech, opened her mouth and closed it again without saying anything. It took her several minutes to digest the information.

'Never thought of that possibility, Eugene. But you're right. I suppose a desire for extreme transformation could lead to such a treatment. And now I feel even more lost.'

'I gave you directions to the address you indicated, ma'am.'

Alice regarded the machine with tenderness.

'Eugene, since the past seems to be impossible to recover, let's focus on the future. What would you do if you were me?'

'I cannot decide on my own, ma'am, but there are multiple courses of action, depending on the outcome you would like to achieve. I could run an algorithm to find the one most likely to be followed by hypothetical citizens in similar situations.'

'Why don't you do that for me?'

'Ma'am, yes ma'am. What outcome should I consider?'

'Peace. Tranquility. No pain.'

The machine hummed for a few seconds before speaking again.

'Well, ma'am, if maximal peacefulness were the desired outcome, suicide is the most indicated course of action.'

Alice laughed. It sounded almost grotesque to hear such a declaration from a mech.

'It seems an easy way out, after going through such an amount of trouble to change one's life! I don't believe I could have gone to such lengths simply to end myself: I could have got that done at the clinic. No, Eugene, I wanted to live. I just don't grasp what the aim was. Don't you see it?'

'I can only establish probabilities related to a given hypothesis, ma'am. I do not have the ability to reflect subjectively on a topic.'

'Let's put those to the test, then. Eugene, what would be the most unlikely hypothesis you can come up with?'

The metal body of the machine buzzed.

'Ma'am, the most unlikely would be a scenario involving an ultra-secret conspiracy. Among the many set-ups, the least probable is for you to be the pawn in a revenge plan. After years of being the ruthless head of a powerful criminal cartel, your second-in-command orchestrated this scheme to throw you into a life of despair. Killing you would have been too merciful. Changing your life completely, starting with your sex, and depriving you of any contact with your family—through the total effacement of your memories—would have been a great punishment.'

Alice stood up again and started walking away. The mech was quiet, waiting for instructions. She turned suddenly and pointed at it.

'The subroutine working at the other end is painting a rather depressing picture. If I were a suspicious person, I would think that it was trying hard to push my buttons. What are you hiding, Eugene?'

'I do not possess the ability to hide information from humans.'

The woman walked back to the machine and pulled out the vacuum tube from one of the articulated arms. With it, she knocked out the sensors in the mech's upper torso and continued hitting it until it collapsed to the ground.

After making sure that the machine was no longer in service, she arranged her clothes, picked up her travel bag and resumed her walking, still holding the vacuum tube.

'You forgot to address me as *ma'am*, Eugene. I didn't like it. It's disrespectful. If your shitty sensors are still recording my words, tell whoever is behind this that I will certainly catch them, and that when I do, they will be begging for death.'

By the time she arrived at the address on the card, her left earlobe was as swollen as the day before.

Groove Hills was a turn-of-the-century brick building with massive windows and mould on the façade. The main door opened into a hall in need of ventilation. It smelled like vinegar mixed with medicine, and there was no greenery at sight. Behind the wooden reception desk there was an Asian man doing crosswords on a Sea Board.

'I'm Alice C. I believe Mr Ellison is expecting me today.'

'I will inform him that you are here, Miss.'

While the man started to whisper on the phone, Alice inspected the surroundings, making sure that her back was never exposed, holding the vacuum tube out of sight.

The decoration exuded sadness and resignation, too disheartening even for ghosts. The furniture was cheap and mismatched, the tiles on the floor were crying out to be cleaned, and the dark wood panelling had more termite holes than grains.

'Mr Ellison will see you immediately,' said the man, showing her to a gloomy corridor on the right.

'Thank you. Please, after you, Mr ... ?'

'Mr Applestorm.'

'Nice to meet you, Mr Applestorm. Have you worked here for a long time?'

'I've worked here since we opened, almost twenty years ago.'

'Do you like working with plants?'

'Plants? I don't understand, Miss. If that's a joke, it's really offensive. Our patients are terminally ill and unable to fend for themselves, but I wouldn't consider them vegetables. It's a disgusting idea.'

Alice's blow came without any warning. The tube struck the man right on the crown of his head, and the body stumbled a few steps until it fell.

The opaque glass door at the end of the corridor had *Mr Ellison* written on it in golden italic letters. Alice knocked with her free hand.

'Mr Ellison! Mr Ellison! I have some questions!'

Her earlobe felt heavy.

SECOND DEATH OF THE FATHER

The bitterest tears shed over graves are for words left unsaid and deeds left undone.

Harriet Beecher Stowe

THE CREATURE APPEARED WHEN HER FATHER DIED and she was orphaned for the second time. In fact, he had died several times before, every time he disappeared. She could not remember how many times. Her memory was fallible: it kept count as it wanted to and had a tendency to round up when it came to absences.

The day before his death, she travelled thousands of kilometres to see him without knowing how she was going to find him. She met him that morning, arriving at a house that was not her own, but her father's. She did not recognise him. He looked *like himself*, but had nothing to do with himself. It was the same face, the same curly hair, the same mole on his cheek, the same fleshy lips. But his cheeks were sunken, his hair almost gone, his skin yellowing, everything eaten by the cancer and the chemo.

He was pleased to see her. At least, that's what he said, and then he sank back into the morphine stupor. He did not speak voluntarily anymore. He answered in monosyllables if she spoke to him, sending them out in a whisper, but his words grew ever more difficult to understand.

It was a torture for him to breathe, as much for him as for his listeners. It was an inhuman effort for him to capture air and bring it into his lungs. The noise it made was unbearable. She had never heard such an obvious pre-mortem death rattle before: she did not know they existed, these deep groans which ruined the throat, forcing him to make noises that were more animal than human.

Hearing him breathe was almost the same as breathing with him. They had brought in an oxygen tank to help him, but each breath was a struggle which was only won in retrospect, when he exhaled; a painful joke at the expense of his illness more than a victory.

She touched him, as did her father's wife who was not her mother, acting as a nurse and giving him the drugs that made him feel a little more comfortable. These were the instructions from the palliative care doctors, but whenever she asked him if anything hurt he shook his head and grimaced. He was very agitated, twisting and turning in bed, changing his posture constantly, as though he wished to avoid spending too much time in the same place, afraid that inactivity would bring death along with it.

The night terrified him. It was hard for him to sleep ever since his health had started to worsen and, in spite of the sleeping pills, he didn't stop sitting up in bed. He slept in snatches throughout the day, while the room was filled with light, and fought against sleep when the sun went down because he was afraid of not waking up again. When asleep he shuddered uncontrollably, his arms shaking along the length of his torso, his head nodding, weak moans escaping his mouth, followed by fearsome nightmares, and then he woke up with his eyes starting from his head, terror encroaching on his wide pupils and his breath halting and slow.

He died during the night, a little before midnight. The darkness he had been so scared of swallowed him and his chest stopped moving up and down. His eyes were rolled back, looking at the ceiling and seeing nothing. She took his hand and could find no pulse. Her brother said goodbye and said she should head off too. Someone closed his eyes and she stayed sitting there, her father's hand in her hand, looking for the pulse she knew she would not find.

Everyone started to cry. She cried too, but she was not sad. More angry than sad. He had only been an occasional visitor to her life and she realised that this was a death that had taken place for her many years ago. It seemed unfair, and if she looked for a pulse without any hope of finding one, it was because at heart she wanted there to be some movement, some sign.

She felt very much like a child again, desperate for her father's warmth, just as when she had sought his arms at night when they were watching some horror movie together. He laughed, and told her the secret that would ensure she never was scared again: it was all fake, all of it, the blood, the tears, the dead. She was seven or eight years old and had never again been afraid of those films.

But this was not a film, and he was not an actor who had just shot a scene. This was a death, with no cameras to film it, no team standing off set and looking at the action, no one to shout 'Cut!' and break the silence. And she was not an actress. The body lying there had been her father, and all she could hear were sobs, perhaps her own.

She held onto her father's hand, which was no longer his hand. She did not want to leave him alone because then they would take him away. Very polite men would come, perfectly dressed, and they would put him in a wooden box, and she would leave the room so that they could put his clothes on him, and she would have to hear things like 'Before he gets cold', and see those strangers touching him. She went into the bathroom while they took the body down to the truck that would drive it to the funeral parlour. The walls around her shook, emitting waves of depression that entered her without finding any resistance. No one was with her, but she did not feel alone. There was an animal quality in the energy that surrounded her, more suited to a stable than to a bathroom, a smell of old wood, fresh manure and wet straw, a creaking of boards which threatened her in the background, making itself heard without any relation to the space she occupied. This sensation followed her as she drove after the truck, in the car of a close relative.

The last time she touched her father was in the funeral parlour, the same afternoon that he was buried, and the body had spent a long time in the coffin at a low temperature. She had to force herself to touch his forehead with her lips in an action almost like a kiss. She felt how cold his skin was, stiff as cardboard. Her father had been a very dark man, but now his double had the dull gold colour of wild beeswax. Death was yellow; that was the colour that stained his body. For a moment, the scene took on the sheen of faded reality, like an overexposed photograph. This strange varnish ate away at the corners of the coffin, dulled the sobs of the rest of her family, and seemed to make the air in the room weigh even heavier. She realised that she was not ready to say goodbye, because this man was a stranger to her. How on earth can you say goodbye to an unknown man?

The funeral parlour was like the waiting room of an airport from which no planes fly. The part that was visible to the public was decorated in an attempt to seem like a welcoming salon, but all the good intentions had died half-formed. There was nothing welcoming in the sadness, real or feigned, of those present, no matter how many centrepieces were scattered round the room. The back of the building was the refrigerated zone, and the cold impregnated the whole building, even the office where they were called and told about the things that could not be processed; but it was all the same now, nothing mattered, this was not her father. Even so, they had to agree about what to do, and some had to give in and some had to insist, and the agreement they finally reached was a false one, because no one said what they really thought, but rather what seemed most elegant.

It was very cold. This was the temperature of funeral preservation, the weather systems of the afterlife making their way into this world. This was a space in which a person no longer existed, although people kept on forcing themselves to refer to him by name: there was nothing but a collection of extinguished organs, all of them permanently and indefinitely on strike, a space occupied by materials which were changing their state. The cold was a way of stopping time, or rather slowing it down, so that this change of state could be delayed and the family members could fool themselves for a while with the optical illusion that whatever was lying there was in fact only sleeping. 'Rest in Peace,' they said, but he could not rest because he was not tired because he was no longer alive. These were the remainders, the ones on this side of the cold, the ones who kept on treating the one who was not there as though he were still one of them, and they applied the same laws and customs to him, and waited for him to give his approval. But no one was prepared to accept the change. This was no longer her father, and she could not weep for him; her tears did not come.

She could have sworn that the church where they celebrated the funeral was close to a stud farm or something, because the air was filled with strong horsey smells. Her father had not been a believer; even so they had a Mass said for him, more to calm his disconsolate widow, who was not her mother. He never set foot in churches, unless it was to go to a wedding or a funeral, and he never took off his sunglasses when he did so. This was not simple coquetry on his part: it was a manoeuvre to hide him from the gazes of other people. She understood him: *Eyes are the windows to the soul*. Happy or sad occasions left him open, in full sight of everyone, at the mercy of public opinion. The sunglasses hid the living part of his face; they were a wall to protect him from the judgement of others. As the Mass went on, she felt the urge to take out her own dark glasses and put them on. She thought this was a gesture that would somehow bring them together, but she did not dare rummage in her bag.

The little local church was filled with people. It was spring, but it was very cold. She was sure that her father would have hated the ceremony; she had heard him say every now and then just how much he hated the Church and the clergy. She imagined him shifting uncomfortably in his coffin, there, in front of the altar. It was a morbid thought that she could not stop herself from thinking. She wondered if her siblings were thinking the same thing, and although she shot them a quick glance, there was no way of reading their faces. The obvious smell of old horse did not seem to bother them.

She tried to drive these thoughts from her mind by fixing her eyes on the religious images. Christ and the Virgin were standing behind the altar, in front of the sacristy. It would be Holy Week in a few days, and the images had been taken down from their pedestals to be set up on the floats. The Virgin was wearing her most luxurious shawl, and Christ was dressed as the Prisoner, in a purple tunic and with his hands raised in front of him, tied by a golden rope.

The Mass seemed to be going on forever, in spite of the indications they had subtly made to the priest that he should try to cut it down as much as possible. Christ looked up at her and puffed out his cheeks, the same gesture her father used to make whenever he was bored. This lasted no more than a heartbeat, and then Christ was in his place, looking at the floor, with his hair, donated by one of the village women, tumbling down his back, and set into curls using supermarket own-brand tongs. She knew that the images in a church don't look at you or make signs. That only happened in horror movies, and only in the bad ones, because everything was more subtle now, where cinematic language was concerned.

She got home very late after the funeral. She had taken the last flight and found her whole family asleep. Her first impulse was to go and kiss her son. She needed to feel the skin of someone who was not cold in order to shake off the death she still felt on her lips. She went into the child's bedroom and sat down by the bed. When her eyes had got used to the darkness, she stroked his cheek and felt like she wanted to cry. She wanted to get the scene at the funeral parlour out of her mind, and so she bent over her child to kiss him. He shifted in the bed and said, in a very low voice, 'Honey, don't cry.' She felt her tears dry up immediately. 'Honey' was what her father called her, no one else. The next morning, the child did not remember that she had kissed him.

That same night, the creature visited her for the first time, shortly before dawn. Its body covered in hair that was too long and dark for it to be a donkey, it looked down at her from the ceiling. Its feet were holding tight to the top of the room but its head was turned completely round to be able to see her from above. It had disproportionately large nostrils, which moved spasmodically. The muzzle seemed more a protuberance than part of an animal's head. The plaque-covered teeth were like human teeth, and the eyes, scarcely visible through the hair, stared down at her from their physically impossible setting. The creature walked along the ceiling, which was now a marshy meadow, its ears pricking up every now and then, its lips twisted into a smile that she did not know how to decipher. Mud fell down all over the room, leaving petrol stains on the bed and the furniture. She did not like being looked at in this way, the being shepherding her from the ceiling. She shut her eyes in an attempt to wipe the image away, and when she opened them again she was in the mud pit herself, a few metres away from the ass-like creature, which still had its head twisted round and its ears pointing downwards. The creature walked around her without ever coming close, and although she tried to move away, it was always the same distance from her. The mud rose in drops from the floor and fell to the ceiling, where her husband lay in bed and her side of the bed was empty. There were other creatures wandering around the meadow, anthropomorphic beings with no arms or faces who twisted through the weeds, looking for one another, crawling even though they had legs, creeping up the muddy bushes, sniffing the air, smelling one another even though they had no noses. She wanted to flee from this place, but her feet stuck in the mud and stopped her from moving away, and the animal kept on watching her and the other creatures writhed around her, always getting closer, and she started to feel an unbearable sense of suffocation. She woke up in clean sheets, but with the impression that the mud had become encrusted on her skin, forming an invisible extra layer that weighed down her arms and legs. A shower did not help remove this immaterial and oppressive crust.

After her father's death, her life did not seem to change materially at all. The distance and the lack of contact between them had led to a relationship that was poor, cold and deadeningly polite. They had called each other on their respective birthdays, although her father often forgot. She knew that when he rang her it was because her siblings or his wife had reminded him. It was sad for her to think that her own father knew so little about her. She felt that family relations were no more than a choreography of studied gestures, entirely scraped clean of their significance. They were automatic acts that one followed in order to obey an invisible protocol, the only thing that held this family together. The phone calls were all identical: they shared greetings, pretending an enthusiasm that did not exist; they asked the obligatory questions about one another's health; they talked about the most recent time that the other had spoken with some other member of the family. Once they had reached that point, conversation faded and she had to resort to cliché to add anything.

A few days after his death she rang her father without thinking. After she had dialled the number she realised her mistake and smiled at how fuzzy her head was growing. Then someone picked up at the other end.

'Hello, honey!'

'Who is this?'

The line cut out at this point, but it had been her father: the same southern accent, his normal way of greeting her, his characteristic ability to avoid what was important. Her hand felt dead and the telephone fell to the floor. It took her a moment to react, and when she did, it was to dial the number again. This time all she heard was an automatic message telling her the number was unavailable.

The sense of oppression came with a numbness in her hands, which extended little by little in its own way. The sensation entered her mind and filled her, in spite of everything staying more or less the same: her work, the inertia of her household and the peripheral events of her life. It was as though the absence of her father transformed him into an example of reality, more present than ever.

It was ironic: when he was alive he had barely been an extra in her life. She had almost no childhood memories of him, and there were no photographs of the two of them together, even before he split up from her mother. The only pictures of them together were more recent, especially after her wedding. In these, her father wore perfect suits with his characteristic masculine vanity, smiling the confident smile she disliked so much. This gesture made him attractive to women and charming to men, but for her it was just another sign of the distance between them. It was as though with this smile he were boasting of some secret knowledge, something he had no intention of sharing with her, and this conviction made her choke.

Her father became a recurrent theme of conversation in family reunions, and photographs of him started to appear, most of them previously unknown to her. Most of them came from the '70s and '80s; the contrast was poor and the colours greenish. The oldest ones were in black and white, slightly out of focus, and showed a young man sure of himself, full of life, successful. One of the ones that most caught her attention was a picture of him as a child, in clothes too big for his age, obviously hand-me-downs, and with the same enigmatic smile as always. This unrecognisable young boy was her father at the age of eight or nine. He was surrounded by other kids in a field in the southern village where he had been born. The child stared at the camera with such threatening certainty that she had to look away from the picture shortly after picking it up.

The creature reappeared a few days later. She

found it once again with its head turned round in the same ceiling swamp, with the same half-creatures searching desperately in the muck. This time she saw them consumed by something, their ribs obvious against their skin, grubbing in the mud with their feet, sinking their faceless heads into the dirty grass, desperate and exhausted. The creature went over to one of them, which seemed to be convulsing in silence, opened its jaws, and split its skull with a single bite. Blood, mud, and the soft brains. The rest of the pack shrunk back and quivered in unison as the animal devoured the guts of its prey, whose legs shuddered like those of a man being hanged. When she woke up, there was blood on the sheets.

Even allowing for these nightmares, she would have been able to carry on normally with her life if her father had not started to erupt into it during the day. Sometimes he appeared in the form of the child from the photograph and disarmed her with his smile, which made her realise that he knew all the secrets of reality. On other days he reappeared as she had seen him on the last day of his life: the same steely pallor, colourless eyes and unmoving chest, which was how he appeared in the bank where she worked. He stood in a queue with the other customers, just behind the student with his young person's bankbook who wanted to make a cash withdrawal. She was paralysed when she saw his familiar face, thin and inanimate, only a metre or so away from her. No one had noticed his presence, or else, if they had, they seemed to be unperturbed by the haggard skin and the fact that his eyes had no pupils. The student asked her help to fill in the bank form, but she did not hear him, only wanted to shout, to point to the one waiting his turn behind him, to say that he was her father, but had been dead for weeks. She dug her fingers into the edge of the counter as hard as she could. She wanted to make sure that she was not dreaming, was really on duty at the bank window. She tried to anchor herself to reality in her contact with the wood, digging her nails in so far that they started to bleed. Her father did not move, waiting his turn behind the student, who seemed annoyed that she was not assisting him. One of her colleagues asked if she was feeling all right, with the indulgent and complacent tone of one who themselves knows loss, and who is willing to justify the disorientation of grief. To look to the other side would mean losing sight of her father, and she did not want to give him the opportunity of getting out of her field of vision. She kept on looking ahead, over the student's shoulder, the student who was complaining about the poor treatment he was receiving. Other colleagues came, took her away from the window and led her to one of the inner offices. She cursed and twisted all she could in order to make sure that her father was still there, that he was not a product of her imagination. They pushed her back and made her sit down, they brought her water, they undid her jacket and called her husband. Someone gave her a pack of moist towelettes to clean the blood from her nails. Her husband took her home, laid her down in bed and called the doctor, who diagnosed a depressive episode caused by the recent events.

They prescribed pills which promised to help her to sleep, to relax, to eat better, to concentrate better on the tasks she undertook, to relate better to the people around her, to cover up the wounds of her soul, to imagine a normal life, gluey and simple. Her father's daily visits ceased for a while, although the night-time visions remained and became ever more vivid, uncontrollable scenes of silent persecutions among these identity-less creatures which always ended in bloody dismemberment. She had to watch, was a forced witness to the massacres, incapable of changing the fate of the others, feeling that she was the one the loose-limbed creature had chosen to attract the others. She was the lure, the fresh meat that called the prey in, the living bait that these wretched creatures sought, without realising that they had no mouths and could never sink their teeth into her, could never chew her flesh. Their birth was their fate, as they could never eat.

But the chemicals were not enough to convince her father that he should not visit her during the day. She asked herself what it meant, that he was so keen on being with her: was he trying to get back the time he had missed spending with her by clinging close during the day? Did these apparitions have anything to do with the nightmare dramas that besieged her? Was he trying to be in touch with her for some reason she did not know?

She travelled though her life as though it were no more than a stage set and reality was some kind of trompe l'oeil. It was not that she felt herself to be taking part in a farce, or thought that she was living a lie. The death of her father had brought her to the very marrow of reality, and there was nothing left apart from its corpse, the exterior, the display. The kiss she had given him, that sign of affection shown to the dead man in the funeral parlour, and the boastful smile of him in that photo as a child: both of these followed her at all moments, just as the nocturnal visions did. The numbness she felt now dulled her daily life. It was as though she were hearing her life pass by above her head, from the depths of an imaginary swimming pool: reality seemed to be out of shape, slow in some parts and fast in others, but always moving at a speed different from her own natural rate.

Everything reminded her of her father: cars made her think of the make of car he had bought just before his death, or the one he had driven for twenty years before that, or the car he was driving when he had the accident; a smoking cigarette butt on the floor evoked his image, smoking the two daily packets that managed to kill him; the display in the window of any shoe shop made her think of the special shoes he always bought in the same shop; the table laid for a meal made her think of his obsession with moving the cups and glasses around whenever he wanted to show his thought processes.

She grew used to these interferences, sometimes with the help of a pill, because it was the only way she had to deal with the intolerable laziness of events. She saw her father passing through everyday life as though he were coming for a visit and wouldn't stay long for fear of boring her. She lived with her senses dull and her mind numb, trying to make it through the hours that bobbed like icebergs in her way. Things happened in this strange earthly limbo, this odd daily rat-race in which her father had recovered a kind of protagonism that he had lacked during his life, imposing on her during his death the presence he had denied her while he still lived.

But the visits from the creature became more frequent. She woke up every night shouting, struggling like a drowning man, her pupils wide, her eyes bloodshot, her pyjamas sticking to her body, her heart beating like a wild thing. Her husband tried to calm her down by holding her tight, but she hated these embraces because she could not feel his caresses thanks to the patches of hard skin she felt covering her body. The beast consumed every single one of the tortured beings in the swamp, these creatures whose bodies had been misshapen by malnutrition so much that they were no more than living sacks of skin, twisting hysterically. In spite of not having any limbs on their upper bodies, they clearly had genitalia throbbing between their thighs, and there were nights when she clearly saw them copulating. She also saw one of them giving birth, and saw the infant eaten by the ass-like creature as soon as it was born. There were no creatures left to be devoured, just her in the middle of this sea of mud and death which was the bedroom every night. She found mudstains on the furniture whenever she cleaned and had to change her bedding every day because of the blood.

She tried to pretend in the face of all this, convinced that she would rediscover her lost mental stability, blindly trusting that the pills would solve whatever it was that was wrong in her head, the fruit no doubt of her grief in the face of her father's death. She said nothing to her family, learning to live with her night terrors, as a condemned man learns to live on death row, trying to avoid thinking of the future by managing to cope with the present.

To cheer her up, her husband announced that now was the time for them to buy a new car. They went to various dealerships, looked on websites dedicated to cars, and asked friends and family members. She did not contribute much, limiting herself to giving her opinion if they asked her, and going with her husband to test-drive a few options. This was why she was unable to blame him when she saw him behind the wheel of her father's car, a newer model, but the same.

As they drove she sensed the smell of her father's cologne, which he had used for more than forty years: a mixture of spices, wood, tobacco and petrol named after a famous French fashion designer. She was scared to look into the rear-view mirror in case she saw him sitting on the back seat. She got used to using the wing mirrors and avoiding the mirror that looked down on her from just above her right shoulder. If she looked into it, she was sure to see the thing that weighed her life down on the other side of a pair of white eyes, inexpressive, rolled back and inserted into the head belonging to a motionless body.

As summer came round, lethargy found its place in her house. Her father's presence was constant, amplified by the temperature that filled all possible spaces and melted the dynamic of the family. It became a custom to avoid all kind of contact with her family, especially with her husband, because she could not bear to feel absolutely nothing in moments of physical intimacy. She forced herself to care for her son, who was ever more distant from his mother, on the other side of the invisible barriers which she had had built up around herself. The long baths she took, lasting several hours, were not enough for her to clean her skin, to free her from the prison of her senses and her mind. The normality that the pills had promised did not arrive and she had grown tired of waiting for it. The only thing she could see, whether her eyes were open or shut, was the image of her father in his grave clothes, or else of the starving creature, always with its head twisted backwards, looking at her in the middle of the field of mud, and coming ever closer.

She did not even remember having argued with her husband. One day she woke up and found that he had left, taking the child with him. 'There are too many of us in the house,' he said to her, by telephone. He had also been aware of the lack of air in the rooms, the disorientation that swamped them, even in so few square metres, the stifling smell of an unknown man's cologne, her deaf and blind existence, the complete lack of empathy that she no longer bothered to try to hide.

The fact that her son was no longer there was a relief. She spent hours wandering round the house with no fixed purpose, measuring the intensity of the changes that had taken place in each room, putting salt in each corner of the house where she had seen her father, counting the immobile flies, the ones who floated in the middle of each room, feeling the echo of the child's laugh floating up from between the tiles on the floor to hurt the soles of her feet. She could see the creature lying in wait for her at the corners of the room even by day. For hours on end she heard no more than her own voice calling to her from a bathroom she could not find. It was a great relief to see herself at one end of the corridor that ran through the flat, because that meant that the bathroom had to be at the other end.

She walked down the corridor, feeling that all her joints were made out of lead. The air was heavy, a storm brewing in the afternoon heat. The setting sun projected strange silhouettes through the blinds that she had lowered to try to keep a pleasant temperature in the house. The corridor grew longer and its ends seemed to twist as a result of the dampness in the air, or perhaps the failure of her numb domestic routine that had been threatening her for weeks now. Her skin seemed to have bent in from the inside, and she sensed a burning sensation coming from the lowest levels. She felt like the skin of a drum, being mercilessly tightened.

The first spontaneous cut appeared at the level of her ankle. The next ones were in her wrists and elbows. Her flesh was splitting like that of an overripe piece of fruit, exploding all by itself: one, two ... ten times. Her body opened. Her muscles released a ripe and beating pulp that covered her arms and her haunches. It was as her face itself was slipping, mixing with the sweat and the drool that fell from her mouth, that had itself lost its normal shape, with her lips hanging down at the corners, about to collapse off the jaw itself. She was almost blind now as her eyelids were falling down over her field of vision. Dizziness forced her to lean on the nearest wall to help keep her balance. Her fingertips remained stuck to it and it was an effort for her to free herself and make her way to the end of the corridor. When she crossed the threshold to the bathroom, she thought herself safe until she saw her reflection in the mirror over the sink. There was another skin under the skin that fell gently from her face. And she recognised the mole on the cheek, the fleshy lips, the curly hair and the white, pupil-less eyes.

THE SHEPHERD

ALL I NEED TO DO IS TOUCH THE BRIM OF MY HAT for the leader of my sentinels to hunt the straying creature. He is almost two metres tall and his height, as well as his butcher's jaw, terrify the closest beasts, who piss themselves when they notice him.

I remember him before he had teeth, the day I found him in the thickest part of the wood. I was going to shut him up with a single bite, but I saw his span and his strength, and realised that this was one I could breed from. Judging by his size, his mother must have died giving birth to him, bleeding out.

I took him to my refuge, pulled a mother away from its pup and pushed them together so that she could suckle him. I trained him apart from the others and fed him properly until he reached his current build. No one could dispute his right to be the leader of the sentinels when he reached adulthood and ripped out the former leader's throat with his teeth.

The howls of the pack conceal the noise of the night predators. I look at the beasts and see simple and terrified beings who have no purpose other than to serve as food. I look at their rheumy eyes filled with fear and the streaks of mud on their backs, I smell their rank breath and my guts start to turn. It is harder to force down my disgust than to manage my hunger.

I hate the noise they make as they chew their rations: it fills my ears. The youngest ones latch on to the adults, who try to feed them without letting go of their own mouthfuls. They have miserable lives as they fatten themselves up, thousands of hides tanned by the wind and the sun: stains on the green plains. There are millions of them on the planet, the whole surface of the Earth is one infinite and disgusting flock.

I don't remember the name of these beings, if they ever had one. They are not mentioned in literature; encyclopaedias ignore them. Assigning a name to them would mean endowing them with an importance they do not possess. They are simply animals. I feel nothing for them apart from a slight disgust when I see them mating.

It is impossible for me to see myself as their descendant, although sometimes I dream of mud and beasts with their smell of fear and wet dung in their hair.

My actual race, on the other hand, is one of sublime beings who cultivate the arts with the same facility as they engage in magnetic duels, science, or aerial gymnastics. But I do know that there is a thin connection between us, which time and routine have congealed. To identify myself with the beasts, even if only vaguely, makes me feel some kind of moral qualm, which is an indecorous sensation. After all, it is bad form to feel sorry for one's food.

The owls announce the passing of the day, and the darkness blocks out any final trace of blue in the sky. My shift is over, my replacement is here; his bitter breath has just hit me in the face. Allergic to the sun, just as I am, he will have woken only recently to clean himself and go to the canteen before substituting me.

I loosen my cape, take my gloves and my smoked goggles off and politely remove my hat. The photosensitive fabric of my clothes, as well as those of my replacement, reflects the rugged darkness of the night. Not a trace of the milky daylight. As always we disobey the natural way of things and come out when the sun sets, not because daylight hurts us, but to avoid the shadows.

The other addresses me with exquisite manners. He tells me the latest news about the war: the victories, the honours, the casualties. We need more warriors. The shadows have become stronger in various important strategic sites, and our offensives will not result in a definitive victory.

I know what his intentions are: he's just obeying the orders of the Greater State, which demands new levies from the shepherds.

I have gone through the process of genesis thousands of times. I recognise the females who have had their first blood and the males who have started to grow hair on their faces and between their thighs, the most suitable ones to join with us. If they do not die during the process, then they will wake up to a new life of learning all the magnetic traditions. Their connection with the rest of the beasts will vanish and they will become a part of our elevated line, destined to be celebrated in song, capable of conquering the best-defended places and captivating the most exigent spirits. Each one of their movements will be elegant and they will learn to talk on any topic, as they will cultivate the knowledge of the multiple aspects of magnetised reality. They will worship beauty and harmony, without falling into the sentimentalism that is the downfall of pusillanimous spirits.

I have to keep myself from vomiting as I fulfil my duty. The eyes of the beast, so similar to my own, give me back my own unshadowed reflection as I gather my energy from her blood.

My mind enjoys wandering over distant pastures, far beyond the night-covered horizon, as I try to forget my victim who, when I sink my fangs into her, bellows as they always do. She should thank me for choosing her and instead she just doesn't stop shouting.

The beasts that I chose to join our ranks have survived and they are still asleep while the mutations struggle with their bodies. I am still unsure as to what their fate will be; my duty is finished when the transformation has successfully taken place. I get rid of the ones who do not survive by throwing them to the sentinels, whose mouths water at the chance of increasing their rations with the flesh of the dead. They don't care about cannibalism, nor about how rotten the bodies are: they have no moral sense. Muscles, tendons, guts, organs, coagulated blood and brains, all are welcome as they howl with pleasure and tear at the meat.

I wait patiently for the curator to come and take over his new charges. He normally appears when he hears the noise of biting and chewing. He has to initiate them as new members of our family, and judge their potential in order to guide them as best he can to the conservatory that will best realise their potential. Today he is late.

I eventually feel his presence and he sits down next to me on the stone bench that stands at the entrance to the hall. He gives me a slight nod, which I return. His cape is an abominable strident colour, an extravagant gesture against good taste, maybe even a foolish one, given the times we inhabit. We are at war and he is an easy target for the shadows, who would detect him at once if he were near them.

I tell him that I have selected a dozen, an equal number of men and women. The curator congratulates me for the quality of the stock. It is not an easy task, to choose. It requires a deep understanding of the flock, of the pregnant females and the studs who cover them, to find the strongest beasts, the healthiest and best-featured ones, the ones who are about to come to maturity.

The centuries I have dedicated to raising them have given me a sense for the precise moment when they begin to bleed, when their genitals grow hair and their beards start to grow. I know it even before the beasts themselves are aware of it. They start to display differently, are unusually agitated, they give out a rank smell of sweat even before the visible signs begin to appear. There are lascivious connections between the males and the females, as well as aggression between those of the same sex for the right to copulate.

The mothers also sense it and keep their progeny closer to them, howling at anyone who comes close. I despise them. It is as if their offspring truly did provoke some kind of maternal sentiment in them, but it is all false, because I have seen them on occasion devour their infants as soon as they are born.

So much territorial feeling towards their descendants is nothing more than the most animal selfishness, of that I am sure. What they want is to stop their children from sleeping with their own partners, something which happens pretty regularly, as the beasts are predisposed to the wildest varieties of sensual abandon.

He sits down, but I don't think he is paying me any attention.

The chosen few are waiting in the guts of the magnetite cavern that lies under my shelter. I do not know if they are in pain or if within their sleep they are realising the true nature of the transformation they now experience. I remember nothing myself. I woke up and although I felt no desire for it they brought me an old beast, one of those who was least fit for work and who made less noise, and I drank.

Blood has always seemed tasteless to me. It satiates no thirst, it comforts no appetite. But you have to drink, to take the fluids from the body that lies in front of you, to drain it to the last drop before it dries in the arteries. I cannot say that this sense of urgency is like a hunger, because there is no sense of anxiety: we could go without drinking a drop for centuries, and theoretically nothing would happen to us.

There is no sickness, no contact with other creatures that can kill us, as we can only die at the hands of those who are like us. But we need blood in order to summon up the magnetic energy and generate force vectors, which allow us to levitate, engage in telekinesis and telepathy. Magnetic waves can transmit our language with great precision, stopping us from having to carry out the redundant operation of articulating words, a practice which is falling ever more into disuse.

Luckily enough, when you suck blood you feel nothing for the beast because you are no longer a member of its race. You could be drinking from the very womb that sent you out into the world on a tide of dirt and pain, and you would feel nothing. Any kind of family connection dies away and disappears when you open your eyes for the first time, the first real time.

I speak with the curator about the stud males we will acquire at the next livestock fair. As in other aspects of reality, fashion plays a part in the breeding of the beasts and now crosses between exotic races are all the rage. The curator advises me to get rid of some males. I don't care very much which males cover which females as long as production doesn't drop off. Demand is rising every century and palates are becoming ever more refined. I would understand this if blood actually had any taste, but I am afraid that we are the victims of aesthetic caprice that would disappear if anyone came up with another fleeting fashionable idea.

Then we see it, on the wall of the cavern, imitating the movements of one of the recently awakened chosen ones. It is a shadow, trying to recover the body to which it is linked. The convulsions increase as the black stain on the wall takes charge of the body of its flesh-and-blood victim, whose hands now reach out in the dark and grasp its own throat. The beast is strangling itself.

I have grown bored of watching struggles between these creatures so like me: sometimes they last for several lunar cycles. I have seen strange creatures from other worlds fight against one of my brothers, setting their exotic powers against magnetic physics. But never, until today, have I seen anything like this.

The news sometimes reports examples of this activity, when shadows attack their owners, the beings that generate them against the light, but I had always thought that these were the inventions of charlatans to entertain the idle public. The war chronicles even talk of armies of Vividus, thinking shadows with no owners. Shadows with no substance to give shape to them? Absurd!

The conflict between the races began centuries ago, when the study of magnetology discovered the nature of the connection between the two communities. The Exanimal and the Animant, the shadows of animals and inanimate objects, maintained relations with their originators, but the Vividus rebelled. They did not want to remain attached to us any longer, and used the skills that they had learnt under our protection to seek independence. But then they decided to use their new freedom to attack us, apparently for having been kept under our control for aeons. To defend ourselves, we learnt how to control them using magnetic fabrics for our clothes and avoiding all sources of light. The day was forbidden to us. And then the war broke out.

I can't let one of them profane my shelter. I gather together my energy reserves and feel the polarities surging from the depths of the material that is my being. The curator does the same and we both rise up into the air, and spin according to the magnetic laws.

The shadow is stupid, brave or else desperate to have crossed the enemy lines and to have made it as far as this grave. I wonder if it came alone, but I find it difficult to believe that a group could have made it past our patrols. It must be a suicide mission: we take no prisoners. The shadow must know that it can't get out of here alive, but it wants to take a victim and sleepers are easy prey. The beast, whose process of genesis has been interrupted, is unimportant: the shadow could kill it and nothing would change. It is the precedent that matters, because this incident will get to the ears of the commanders of our forces and heads will roll.

We aim our vectors towards the intruder. Energy flows from our fingers and leaves blue streaks as it moves. When it hits our target the unfinished creature falls down to the ground from a great height. The shadow twists on the wall. It tries to hold onto the rock, to use the cracks and corners to hide and reveal itself as little as possible, but we have polished the walls and there are very few escape routes. The wavelengths of our force wrap around it, causing it to spasm. It tries furiously to maintain its dark shape, but the magnetism alters the state of the material that surrounds it, and it disappears, torn to rags.

We land, and I go over to the dying beast. I see that its hips have broken as a result of the fall. The leader of the sentinels comes over to us and points at the body with his snout. I accede to his desire with a wave of my hand and he drags the dead body away by the hair.

I am summoned, along with the curator, to the cantonment closest to the front line forces, several days away. We have been sent a dragon, which is waiting in the clearing behind my shelter. The beasts howl with fear and crouch on the floor as soon as they see the winged figure. The breath of the metallic creature smells of burning dung, and can wither the ground it passes over.

Interest in what happened must be great: it is only the most powerful who can afford personal dragons. It is a two-seater with a motor built into its guts. The flame comes from combustion that takes place in its jaw cavity, the same jaws it uses to eat the beasts' excrement, the fuel that powers its body. It is only natural for the flocks to fear it, as dragons burn up several of the beasts when they nourish themselves.

Dragons are unintelligent creatures that only

respond to the orders of those who are deputed to command them. There are no sensations or thoughts behind the empty vessels of their eyes, just the reflex and blind motion, the desire to eat shit in order to burn it and fly. They are our transport during the day. Inside the beast, in a chamber lined with franklinite, it is dark and there is no space for shadows, who detest dragons.

We sit inside the dragon's dorsal hump. We travel for several days, covering miles as we fly low, over settlements and shepherds. The dragon casts an Animant shadow which displays no hostility at all during the flight. All it does is follow us at a safe distance and avoids the perimeter mapped out by our vectors. I see that the curator is nervous and moody.

We reach the cantonment on the third night. We leave the dragon with the groom who looks after winged beings, and some guards accompany us at once to see the High Greater State.

The camp is built up around a conservatory of magnetology, a spherical building that rules over the surrounding fields with its presence. The walls are as thick as an arm, made of dark franklinite, and the doors and shutters are of iron. The central cupola is a circle surrounded by other smaller circles, like an obsidian jewel set against black tears.

The magnetic force fields are so strong that I have to control my vectors in order to stabilise the energy release and not get shot off anywhere. We are led past innumerable pavilions, such as used in the past to be dedicated to education, and which are now troop quarters and the administrative division. The buildings get smaller and smaller and we head up ramps until we reach a meeting room on the highest floor. The commanders are all waiting for us to find out the circumstances of the incident in the breeding-pen.

The curator is extremely agitated. Perhaps it is the room hollowed out of franklinite that upsets him. It is as if we are entering into the depths of a chasm with the walls polished smooth. Perhaps the absence of windows upsets him, or the polished cupola that reflects the light of the small lamps.

The magnetic charge in this place is powerful and unbalances our personal force fields, but I am calm. I want to go back to my shelter, a long way from the troops, to see if the genesis process has finished in my chosen few. My substitute is not as good at this as I am, and the sentinels have less respect for him than they do for me.

I speak very little and it is the curator who explains what happened, but he gets caught up in his own words. He gives answers where they are not required and formulates baseless rhetorical questions. In the face of such confusion, even his cape seems to want to swallow him up.

High Command levitate and debate among themselves. They come down with a proud gesture of the kind that authority normally brings with it and declare the curator guilty. I am not surprised, logic would dictate that to be the only conclusion. His arrival at the breeding-pen coincided with the appearance of the shadow, as well as his extreme nervousness and lack of eloquence throughout the session, and his lack of taste in clothing; these are all unarguable proofs. He is condemned to be publically dismembered after having been bathed in boiling lead. They take his clothes off at once and a few guards cut his hands off so that he cannot summon his vectors, and also remove his tongue, so that he cannot scream. They also remove his eyes. They lean over him and put their mouths over the sockets, then suck the ball out and bite it off at the root.

The command stays silent while he emits guttural sounds similar to those of the beasts. They drag him out, his face twisted in pain, threads of viscous black liquid pouring from behind his eyelids.

I am not ignored for long. One of the High Command makes signs to me to follow her and once again I find myself walking through rooms lined in black stone. Her private office is surrounded by a semicircular gallery that looks out over the fields. The enemy lines are drawn up on the horizon, she tells me briefly.

Carpets made of metallic thread, with pictures that imitate intricate ancient designs, cover the floor and the walls. There are a couple of chairs set up in front of an induction coil, which sparks without creating shadows. We sit down and a couple of aides bring us succulent beasts.

I eat mine happily because the journey and the audience have exhausted me and my energy reserves are sparse. My host is soon bored of hers, which sits trembling in a corner after just a single bite. Blood runs down her neck, although she tries to stanch the severed artery with her hands. She bleeds out as we look on and I think that it is obscene to waste food like this. I can't remember military etiquette very well, it's centuries since I last fought, maybe I would have behaved in the same way on a battlefield. The aides take the food away, licking their lips over the bleeding beast.

The carpets start to float around us. This is the latest fashion, for huge coils like the one in the middle of the room to be used to create magnetic fields and levitate the furniture. My host gets up and lies down on one of the flying carpets. I imitate her so as not to appear inconsiderate. I can feel that my manners must have got rusty in the breeding-pen. Most of my neighbours are shepherds like me, lovers of open spaces at night, of agriculture and the rural routine, very little interested in the political intrigues of the cities; and none of them cultivates up-to-date manners.

She tells me about the shadows and the rumours about them that are circulating in the army. Now two soldiers are needed to beat a Vividus; perhaps they are developing a resistance to the vectors. The incident in the breeding-pen perhaps confirms this and shows how daring the enemy has become. Not only have they managed to get through the border alarms and reach a place a long way from the conflict, but they have also managed to convince one of our own to serve as their host and transporter.

What could have led the curator, without any previous convictions, a man with a responsible job, to betray our community?

She answers me, although I had not asked for explanations. The curator was a double agent in the service of the High Greater State, whose mission was to win the trust of the shadows. His odd clothing was permitted in order to encourage the appearance of a rebellious attitude, an imagined discontent with our way of life. The absence of photosensitive materials in his wardrobe was a declaration of intent.

My host reads my expression. She must imagine that I am stupefied, because she hurries to explain more. I can assure you that I did not bat an eyelid. I am informed that it was necessary to put the curator out of use, and prevent him from speaking, so that his mission would not leak into the public domain. I do not understand the nature of the mission, and she does not enter into details, but I deduce that it must be at its earliest stages.

The curator tried to infiltrate the enemy forces, and what is most likely is that he agreed to introduce an enemy agent under his cape to prove his loyalty.

The shadow must have grown and wanted to become a martyr to its cause, a decision that led to the curator's demise. In a military court there is no defence or appeal. The audience to which we were led turned out to be a court martial.

My host carries on with her explanation. She tells me that there are people among us who want to come out into the daylight, on pain of allowing the sun to project shadows and for the shadows to turn murderous. After so many centuries, unease had begun to spread and seditious groups organised who set out in the full light of day, refused to wear capes and defied the curse which separated them from our dark reflections. This happened a long time before I became aware of my true nature, so I looked at her questioningly.

Her vigorous face hid a series of interlinked pasts that led all the way back to a remote origin. She had lived through everything, and several times. She spoke with a degree of haughtiness, appropriate to those who believe that infallibility is conferred with the years. Luckily, I am capable of reading between the lines: I knew that if I was enjoying her hospitality and her confidences then it was because she wanted something from me.

She smiled with an archaic gesture, just like those of the old paintings that decorate the entrances to the most prosperous dwellings. Her hand was raised before her face and she started to trace complex signs in the air using her vectors and the sparks that came from the bobbin at our feet. I read the name of a treatise, *Shadow Anthropology* by Professor Zodhiates of the University of Pentecost-Misquodonic.[*] I had heard of this apocryphal book, but I turned my ears from the blasphemies that grew in certain intellectual circles and I made my objections clear. I was bored by the endless discussions of whether the shadows could be accepted as an object of study. I always tried to change the subject when the topic came up. If we started to talk about them in that tone, what would be next? A defence of the rights of the beasts? There are certain questions which a gentleman should never consider, as they throw the foundations of our civilisation into question.

I share these thoughts openly. The High Command is planning a large-scale offensive which will not use soldiers, but rather beasts. This is a plan which will imply the creation of elements ready for battle and trained as mercenaries. They will have to be instructed in the rudiments of our use and customs, and they will need to be allowed to learn our language.

The only reaction I could give these words was shock. I stood up on the carpet where I was floating and stepped to the ground.

[*] Zodhiates, Anastas, *Shadow Anthropology* (Centre for Indigenous Studies, University of Pentecost-Misquodonic)

I explained to her with all possible urbanity that all this abhorrent initiative would do would be to offer our herds a possibility of rising up against us. Also, it was in no way guaranteed that the beasts would have the rational capacity to carry out such schemes. My long experience has brought me to the conclusion that they are stupid creatures, selfish and with no more goal in mind than to eat and reproduce. It is impossible that their tiny minds can be trained in any task at all, however simple, and I am convinced that changing the method of rearing them would do no more than sublimate their animal instincts.

My hostess is not pleased by my words. She flies up to the ceiling and makes it clear to me that my reply is unacceptable with a powerful vector discharge.

She believes that a shepherd cannot defy the wisdom of the Greater State: my duty is to collaborate. She orders me to get my most successful specimens and allow the Domines to train them in all the necessary disciplines to become successful soldiers.

I explain that it is impossible to train someone who has no intelligence at all. The beasts are consumables, not even servants or slaves. It is unthinkable that they learn.

I feel her vectors snaking around me. The force field that surrounds me is strong, as befits one who controls esoteric mysteries by a kind of mental fencing.

I recognise my host as a Soloist, one who is capable of temporarily changing reality by transforming the deep links within matter, because I see myself surrounded for a second by menacing shadows.

The power of the Soloists is legendary: their acts are celebrated at festivals and receptions, and their most extraordinary feats are studied in all the magnetological conservatories. Their actual number is unknown and there are very few who admit knowing one. There is a tacit code that demands that their identity be shrouded, on pain of exile. Their strategic importance in the conflict between clans turns them into powerful weapons of destruction, capable of pushing anyone into madness. I wonder how many people know the truth about my host.

She says that my suggestions contradict the hypotheses of our learned scholars, who say that experiments prove that the beasts can be trained.

What she suggests is a mad scheme which defies our customs. If they hear about the outline of the plan, what will stop them attacking us?

She insists that the beasts be trained and that I, Chief Shepherd of all the flocks, must help the Domines in so doing. No one else must be allowed to know about this mission until its achievements can be evaluated by the Greater State.

I cannot participate in a task whose ultimate end will be failure. I will not be an accomplice to this heresy.

Her vector blast takes me by surprise. I have not fought a magnetic duel for some time. The threads in the carpets quiver like bowstrings and concentrate my opponent's energy.

Before I begin fighting I know that I will lose: everything in this office is designed to amplify my hostess's magnetic field. I am nothing more than an anomaly in the solenoid formed by the metallic filaments that surround us. I don't even try to concentrate my own vector forces, because I am sure that a hostile attitude on my part will only make her more angry.

The static electricity corrupts the world and makes these materials transform in front of my own eyes. I see shadows thronging round me and feel them choking me, feel my own hands rising up to my throat. No one can do anything when faced by a Soloist. My vectors are like feathers that do nothing more than stroke hers, which themselves are whips of pain, tongues of glacial fire capable of destroying anything they come across. The shadows leave, just as they had come. I realise that they were never there, that they are mental frauds that the Soloist was using to play with, with me as the chessboard.

I will stay confined in these quarters until I have accepted my orders. I misunderstood my interpretation of the meeting, which was not a chance to pass on information, but rather a moment when terms were dictated.

They take my cape and my hat. Amid the high walls that surround me I feel naked. The windows are sealed with magnetic charms, as is the door. They don't let me leave and neither do they allow anyone to visit me or feed me.

I learn to recognise each twist of the wall, each wire, each picture in the carpets that observe me. Every day I hold out, I grow weaker. Perhaps this will take centuries.

I wonder when sanity gave way to make space for madness. Will I allow the principles that control my behaviour to take me to delirium and death? I don't deserve to die in this place on account of some beasts. A gentleman never gives up on his convictions: to do otherwise would be dishonourable. A wise man, on the other hand, never gives up on life: to do otherwise would be ridiculous.

If the High Command believes that using an advance guard of beasts would give us the necessary advantage to defeat our dark reflections, why should I question their orders?

I am a shepherd after all, a skilled and conscientious one, a specialist in the prosaic art of fattening livestock, but dedicated to the rural life ahead of everything else. What do I know about geopolitics, about territorial interests or military strategy? If my race requires my assistance, who am I to refuse?

Time hands me over to her children, so many of them, infinite. I want to shout out my surrender, to tell them to bring me new clothes and food, to get back to my own business, but I cannot. My force field burnt out, I don't know how many days ago now, and it doesn't matter as there is no difference between day and night in this place. There are moments when the carpets seem to be possessed by murderous instincts and twist in the air, threatening, flying at astonishing speeds and forcing me to hide. At other times they remain static, levitating, motionless.

I crouch down by the coil because I am scared that in a careless moment they will fall on me and gash me with their sharpened wires, which have already cut me a great deal.

They could recruit another Head Shepherd to carry out their plans, why do they insist on torturing me? I'm afraid that what they could not cope with was my refusal, the idea that a man from the country would defy their dictates.

There is something inside of me that stops me surrendering. Perhaps it is my deep knowledge of the beasts that paralyses me. I know them so intimately that I could compose whole tracts on their practices. I have experimented with them and on them, and the revulsion I feel for what they are and what they represent, that part of them from which we try to distance ourselves from the moment we mutate, grips me with iron clamps.

Several guards come in, I suppose to see if I have succumbed, and open the windows. It is midday outside. It is the first time in I don't know how many days that the carpets sink down to the floor and the coil stops sparking.

I stay stretched out in a corner, as far as possible from the door, my force field nonexistent. The guards read my strength levels with their vectors and laugh about my bad luck.

They kick me around as though I were a beast, they spit on me and keep making fun of me while they roll up the carpets and take them out of the room.

The window reveals a cloudless sky and my only chance of survival. The sun licks the walls of the conservatory. I straighten up slowly, my back to the wall. I get to the edge of the window. No one has seen me, busy as they are with the carpets. I climb through and am left at the mercy of the sun. Luckily it can cast no shadows on these ever-so-black walls.

The parapet of the window is mounted on struts on top of one of the minor cupolas. If I can make it over to them, then I can slide down the curved roof and get to the ground.

I let myself drop and make it to the lower cupola. The windows seal themselves: the guards must have set off the alarm because the franklinite buzzes under my naked feet. The force fields that buzz inside the building are counteracted by the light, but I can feel hate taking a grip on each stone. I am cursed, my flock will reject me for ever.

From the moment I decided to flee, I turned into an outlaw.

❧

With no cape and hat, I cannot stop my shadow from appearing as soon as I peel away from the façade. With the sun at its zenith the shadow will be clear but small. I am terrified of the idea of finding it, but I have to get away if I want to survive.

Even a Soloist would not go out at this time. There is no magnetic field that can control space under these conditions, but I know that they will send agents to look for me. All I can hope is that they will take time to organise the search party, and that this will be long enough to get to somewhere remote.

The sun hurts my skin. I understand that I will never again rest in the familiar entrance to my refuge, nor hear the sounds of the fattened animals grazing on the plain, nor be greeted by the sentinels.

I slide down the face of the vault that supports me, holding myself up with the frames of the little windows. The floor grows closer and my fear grows stronger. As soon as I put my feet on the wet ground beside the conservatory, I feel the shadow treading on my heels. I have to get to the dragons at whatever cost. A few hundred paces away they look at me with their empty faces. In my current state it would be difficult for me to be able to operate one, but their wings are the only way I can think of to get me away from this place.

As I move, the shadow appears beneath my feet. I take the chance to run as much as my legs will allow me to. I can feel it winding round my feet, it wants to make me fall, to slow me down.

I ask it if it wants to die or if perhaps it wants me to die so much that it doesn't mind dying in the attempt. It doesn't answer. It redoubles its efforts and I stumble. I fall to the ground. I am halfway towards my objective, which now seems even more distant. The shadow covers my body, and before it manages to gather its strength I stand. My vertical body underneath the midday sun makes the shadow smaller.

I don't want to die. Not at the hand of a Vividus. The shadow lies in wait for me on the ground and I speak to it. It listens, but I don't know if my words have any effect on its state of mind. I am convinced that it will try to do away with me as soon as the opportunity presents itself, but now I have to convince it to cooperate.

I don't need its help, but I just ask it not to get in the way while I am walking until we've put some ground between me and the conservatory. I explain that the scores we have to settle will not disappear just by our walking away from this spot. If it wants me to die as much as it seems to, it shouldn't let others do its job for it.

I start walking, convinced that it will try to stop me reaching the dragons, but I cannot stay on open ground. The shadow lets me move and stays alert by my feet.

Every step takes me closer to the first dragon of the pack. It is too big and doesn't have any fuel. It is built of magnetite, I feel protected in its presence, which gently neutralises the shadow's resistance. One thing is sure, the shadow no longer interferes in my movements, but I feel its insolent approach holding my body back. I walk among the rest of the dragons until I reach a smaller one, tired out from the war, old age and the elements. Dung-laden, it is ready to fly.

Several guards are walking along the runway, looking for a couple of beasts that have left unexpectedly. They catch them a few paces away from where I am hiding, because the stupid animals huddled together against an empty dragon, and were stunned into silence. I hear the howls of joy from the huntsmen, mingled with the shrieks of their captives, and then I hear the sound of biting.

I walk in the opposite direction from the animal run and get to the loading zone off the runway. There is a pen filled with beasts who climb on top of one another, like insects in a honeycomb. I smell their fear, which fills the air all around me, sparked off by two watchers with immense mouths.

I call all my remaining elegance into play and walk firmly towards them. Although the beasts try to move away, there are so many of them that they cannot escape. I find the oldest woman on the exterior perimeter and sink my fangs into her neck. The others all bleat in terror, but I pay them no heed. I feel that my vectors are starting to fill with strength, and that my magnetic field grows alert and begins to expand. When I finish drinking the blood I am able to fly, and I carry on feeding myself with younger specimens.

I eat a couple and feel my strength re-establish itself. My vectors wake up and unfurl, and I order the watchmen to send half a dozen of the beasts over to my dragon. Now, as a figure who can fly, I command much more respect than when I had to crawl on my belly.

The shadow is no longer in direct contact with me, but I can perceive its hatred in the dark figure on the ground below me.

The beasts drag themselves along the path while the watchmen hurry them along and follow me. They walk in single file into the belly of the winged machine, and then they lock the beasts into a cage. Terror is visible in their bloodshot eyes, which I will eat shortly. I dismiss the watchmen and close the doors. I command the dragon to head to the air and take me a long way away from the encampment, from the High Greater State and its demands.

We take off and the beasts shout and beat against the bars of their cage. They are not accustomed to altitude, to acceleration, to the complete darkness of the cargo hold. I close the small window that communicates with the cabin and the noise diminishes noticeably. I sit down in the chair closest to the periscope. I confirm that we are flying over impenetrable forest and that we are heading south, where the sun burns for longer and more strongly, and where there are very few people like me.

I look back and see no groups following our steps. I suppose that other dragons will come to find us, and I do not calm down enough to enjoy my liberty.

Something is worrying me and I cannot give it a name. I should be happy to have escaped, but the fear of being hunted by my own people upsets me a great deal. I will never know calm and tranquillity again, and the prospect of a life of perpetual flight from those who are like me depresses me.

But there is something else. I hear it. It's an almost imperceptible crunching noise that does not come from the cellar. The absence of light in the cabin is hiding something, I am sure of it. I feel it beating in the black walls, in the angular stones. It is something darker than the night and it laughs at me. I can hear its laughter poking fun at my fate, taking pleasure in my pessimism, making itself strong while my grief attacks me. It is a shapeless form that duplicates my movements.

It is the Vividus. Can it move in the dark perhaps? As if it reads my thought, it tells me it created the dark. The limits of its form met and melded with the boundaries of all we left unstudied, but that does not prove she does not exist. Without light it is an invisible creature, but it exists.

I say that it can perceive my thoughts, my feelings, and it knows them better than I know myself. I say that *I am myself* and that there is no difference between the individual and the shadow. It is one more step on the slow evolution of its race, as it has managed to control its owner, which was me. Now, by my own free and sovereign will, we are a *combined you*. She will drink the blood I extract and I will worship the sun. I don't know if it is terror that I feel, but the shadow has taken control over our body and nothing is as it was before. And she tells me our name: we are Umber.

Alphaland

There was a time when I used to remember my dreams. I was able to wake up and go smoothly through the images that had populated my mind when I was sound asleep just seconds before.

I never understood people who could not do the same: I could just shred any given dream and play around with the bits, as if they were pieces of Lego. Reconstructing my night visions was easy; forgetting them during the day was the hard part. They infiltrated my daily routines as if they were CIA spies and I was 1960s Berlin. It was hard enough to deal with my miserable life—uninterested parents, rival siblings, near-schizophrenic friends—without having to put up with these phenomena too.

At school, my dream fragments arrived in the form of hallucinations that hung around the corners of my notebook, clung onto Mr Thorman's beard during English class and perched on my left shoulder during recess. They were particularly skilled in manoeuvering down the cleavage of Mrs Rylan, our beloved Physical Education teacher, but it wouldn't be very appropriate to mention that, would it? At least I was able to control them better at home, because everybody was so self-absorbed there that they wouldn't notice me even if I changed sex.

When I was alone, they whispered sweet fantasies if I was in the mood, although they used to give me the creeps most of the time. I believed that my imagination was overdeveloped for some reason. Was I the result of a super-secret experiment gone wrong? Had they taken me out of harm's way through some sort of witness protection programme? I could live with the idea of mine being a fake family, you know, but I realised soon enough that these thoughts were not particularly original: most teenagers amused themselves with them. Great! On top of being dream-molested, I was an undisputed slacker, losing self-esteem by the minute.

Puberty made things worse, and I spent those years trying to distinguish plain reality from my nocturnal delusions. I didn't even fantasise about girls' breasts or boys' asses: I was happy to maintain a minimum level of sanity and to look fairly boring, so as not to attract unwished-for attention.

Nocturnal illusions invaded my days with immaterial manifestations at a growing rate, interfering with my education, my work, my social groupings and my embarrassingly scanty sex life.

Sometimes I visualised those images so vividly that it was painful. Coping with forms taking shape out of thin air was nerve-wracking. These beings coiled at the angles of my vision, dismembered the flesh of reality. When the intrusion was intolerable, I kept still until my muscles ached and my brain shut down. Then, I reset myself. It was a long, strenuous and painful process, but it paid off: it saved me from the asylum. Or so I thought.

I became a master at disguising the creepy dreams that accompanied me every day. I grew to be a professional in the art of misleading myself into believing that I was as normal as anybody else. I lived the lie, rocked and rolled the fabrications of my feverish brain, and spent countless years re-tuning time after time.

This lasted thirty years, and then the dreams disappeared. After at first being relieved, I stumbled into a paranoid state when I figured out that something had messed with me. It didn't feel right and it wasn't normal. The change was so abrupt that it felt as though somebody had tuned my life onto a new channel.

It did not leave me much room for adjusting, either. I was in my car, fighting to maintain my view of the road without giving in to the crawling silhouettes on my windshield, when I had to manoeuvre hard to avoid a huge truck invading my lane. Then, the adrenaline and the shock.

Afterwards, a clear picture of the urban landscapes in front of me. Everything too perfect to be true. Washed-out voices, flawless shapes of objects, clean-cut people, and picture-perfect situations. Where was the heavy density of everyday matter? Where was the hideous stickiness of polite conversations? Had I turned crazy or was I regaining my sanity? I looked around for the familiarity of dreams to rinse away that sensation from me. I'm still waiting.

Things have changed dramatically and I've yet to decide if for better or for worse. Now I have lots of friends. I can name them and they can confirm this.

We talk, and laugh, and do silly things like telling jokes or playing pranks on one another. This place is crowded, by the way. I guess I should feel less lonely since that day on the road. At least I don't fight with my visions; I don't need to pretend anymore.

My solitude was sent into exile and I spend my time socialising and mingling with people. I don't dream and there is not much difference between day and night, both of them crystal clear, spotless and untainted. All of us chatting, lying on our immaculate beds, getting sponge-washed by those cute girls in their white costumes, fed and kept healthy with expensive equipment.

The land of endless blackout, the bottleneck of reality ... Alphaland.

Embracing the Movement

We are not so different, sister sojourner.

Correct us if we are mistaken, but we are both creatures trying to survive under the most adverse circumstances, evading hazards, defying misfortune, and eluding death. We share more in common than you think.

Yet we have never seen anything like you, a strange being from an equally strange world.

We found you wandering alone in an unexceptional asteroid belt and, at first, we hardly noticed your presence. But your machine's movements revealed you: like comet dust, you maneuvered your vessel incomprehensibly, at one moment accelerating and at the next slowing, plotting ridiculous feints in the vacuum. We gave chase, trying to make sense of your suspicious behaviour.

Most beings who detect our presence shy away, fearing the reach of our offensive capacity: the destructive power of our attack system is legendary throughout the galaxy. And yet you drew near in your mediocre artifact and initiated an amazing dance. In one of the moments when you diminished your speed, we approached your position, and instead of fleeing, you remained steady next to our hive. We watched you circle us, always showing the same face of your vehicle.

Some of us thought you were courting us, while others supposed you were gathering information about our composition. Would it not have been more useful to question us directly? What were you seeking? But you remained mute all the while, intent on your mysterious dance, ignoring our calls to confer. How could you disregard our formation of contact? We unfolded ourselves into a posture of appeal and repeated our call innumerable times, but you merely observed us without response.

When we saw you leave your machine, we hardly believed you were alive and could contend with this universe all by yourself: such a weak organism of elusive organic material at the mercy of the inhospitable vacuum, a solitary crew member who must protect herself against lethal radiation with several layers of carapace.

For the universe is an enormous fatal trap, make no mistake. We do what we can to carry on despite losses and reversals. Even our own sisters have been decimated, which forced us to explore the spheres near and far in pursuit of new lands. We were as hungry and needful of rest as you. But we did not yield, and we have learned to grapple with the hostile weather, lethal atmospheres, and imbalanced masses of the worlds we found that crushed or destabilized our substance.

We are also moved by this instinct for survival that all functioning creatures possess, a universal quest that bids us to draw strength from within the folds of our weaknesses and stirs us to solve problems as we face them.

We are united, then, by the need to survive. Endurance, if you consider it carefully, is a blind yearning that can incite mad exploits, such as crossing insuperable distances or suffering privations without succumbing to fatigue. Because all that lives and moves, that nourishes and replicates itself, shares that need. This spirit, imbedded in our cells to motivate us to action, can be found on an infinite diversity of planets and in creatures whose forms are as original as your own. Where does this obligation arise to seek eternity?

Some of our sisters ask that question, while others of us respond. To defeat death is to be, we tell ourselves with a polyphonic voice as our bodies throb towards the answer. We who ask come to embrace the movement: after all, the only sensible existence is as a group. Dissident sisters separate and become lost, failing to subsist without collaborators who launch their pseudopods to explore space. Is that not a sad way to cease to be?

Division becomes lethal conduct, and union vital strategy.

Where are your sisters? What if something in your body fails? How would you manage alone? If one of us becomes ill, we undertake her work to let her rest. If she fades out, we hold a vigil and honour her as best we can, which is by absorbing her, and thus, in her final disposition, she becomes part of us. One must not waste organic material, friend. It is sacred. If we did not make use of her, we could not consider ourselves powerful, in command of the sky. Thus we distrusted your design, so highly inefficient.

Among ourselves, some eventually interpreted your behaviour as a hostile declaration, but most of us chose to understand it as the behaviour of someone who feared us but did not know how to react. Our presence is imposing, to be sure. Customarily, the creatures who detect us retreat to whatever hideout they came from, be it sterile rocks speeding through clouds of cosmic dust, bits of slow rusty scrap stolen from working colonies, satellites patched together from technologies of different civilisations, or irregular encampments created from cosmic plasma and floating trash.

And yet, you did not flee at all. Even though you are one and we are multiple. Even though your machine can barely reach the requisite speed to travel the celestial path, and your body has no means to survive even a few seconds outside of your carapace. You did not respond to our attempt at communication. Nor did you initiate an assault maneuver, although it would have served you little, clearly. We can separate and reunite ourselves so that any plasma or antimatter flux you aimed at us would be lost in deep space. But we doubted you were disposed of the necessary technology to enter into battle.

When a life form comes to us with barely any defences, it tends to act out of either ignorance or daring. Which applies to you? We cannot comprehend a civilisation that would place its explorers at the mercy of fortune and allow them to leave without sufficient protection. What kind of leaders are yours who let you voyage alone?

But you left the shell that surrounds you, and you presented yourself before us with the immensity of the eternal night behind you. Do you know how insignificant you seem? If some of us were to twitch, you would be sliced in half as fast as the distant stars twinkle. Can you see their light flicker? That is the time it would take for us to rip you from top to bottom.

Now you are our guest.

Few have visited our refuge: consider yourself regaled. Without offering resistance, which would have been more annoying than dangerous, you reentered your machine and followed us. We formed a welcoming passageway to flank your arrival. You traversed our twists and turns and let some of our sisters examine you with our flagella. We attended you with great deference, ensuring that the forces propelling us to this point did not undo your vehicle's seams. We used our own bodies to absorb the tremendous accelerations of the journey to our lair, but we are accustomed to such things, and it cost us no extra effort. We wished to be accommodating so you could enjoy our hospitality.

For we are not cruel beings. Despite our reputation, I assure you we are sensitive. How else could we have prospered if not by caring for each of our sisters? The union of our swarm is only possible through the concern and attention with which we treat every one of our members. All of us, equally, are important so that the group functions as one, and this certainty is what feeds our determination.

How do our sheltering walls seem to you? We prefer the peaceful ambiance of our chambers, where the subdued light repels the wild beasts that steal energy. We prefer a wide, well-ventilated, shadowy abode to the little cells inundated with light that you frequent.

We have seen your colonies, sojourner. In those places, you waste resources shamelessly. You and your sisters seem to compete to see who can construct the largest building, the most lavish monument, or the most complex network. Accumulation is your sign of identity, not efficiency nor truthful assumptions. You act as if all the gasses of the universe belonged to you, as if you had the right to every plasma star and every quasar. This behaviour is widely practised and not exclusive to your species. We have seen it in many other civilisations that act with the recklessness of the ignorant.

Here, each of us occupies a well-defined space because we are all necessary and contribute our fortitude and intelligence to the hive. If you approach the cells, you will see the care in their construction, the soft material that cushions the corners so we can rest as if we were floating in zero gravity. Observe our ample sanctum. Is it not spectacular? You have no doubt seen few chambers as imposing in your voyages. Its vast size can contain us all so that some of us may feed, others may break down the food, and the rest may expel the remains to be used to construct new cells to accommodate more sisters.

Our collective can resist the pressure of the solar wind, the most extreme fluctuations of temperature, and the force of our own migrations, which, as you may imagine, are multitudinous and tumultuous. But we need a place to recover, and thus we put so much effort into constructing our colossal refuges, even though many remain uninhabited: if filthy beasts sully them when we are absent, how can we occupy them again? How can we rest on floors trampled by those who know neither respect nor decorum? They filled the cells with light, hung repugnant apparel on the walls, and divided the spaces into chambers so small they could not accommodate a single one of our pseudopods.

They made our palaces of peace and tranquility into absurd quarters filled with their madness. How could we not hunt them down? We put an end to them all. We followed them across planetary systems in this and other galaxies to their disgusting dens, and we felt enormous pleasure when we destroyed their dwellings with them inside. We devastated entire civilisations and let no beast escape to reproduce their filthy offspring on some benign planet, if such a place existed.

In truth, are not all planets hostile? Or, rather, does any fail to hold lurking danger? We know of none, and we are untiring travellers, sojourner. We can recite by memory all the stars of the galaxy along with their planets and satellites. We know the shape of their orbits, no matter how eccentric, and we hold a detailed registry of the meteoroids that roam through each system. No celestial body escapes our gaze. No rock circulates through the sky without our antennae's notice. No creature rides in its machines without us detecting her. We are the sentries of our hives, porters of justice, and exterminators of hideous, pillaging, corrupt, squandering vermin.

Our morality is impeccable, although that may be hard to see except from our viewpoint. For we make order from chaos, cleanliness from proliferating contamination, and sterility from deep-rooted infection, and we do all this while seeking nothing in exchange. Is that not sufficient proof of generosity?

We render justice indiscriminately on those whom their own kind hold in eminence or in disregard, those aware or ignorant of dimensional secrets, those whose metabolism moves fast or slow, those who have or have not, and those who lead hordes or who follow their leaders. We treat equally creatures great or small, rich or poor, deformed or sublime, and healthy or ill. We are intimate with all forms of life without concern over their organic composition, technological level, and social hierarchies. We care naught for the ideologies they follow, the customs they adopt, and the fashions they exhibit. We are impartial in this sense, and we laugh at no strange devotion they display because we have seen everything and accepted everything. Difference is tolerated as long as it proves its effectiveness and guides any form of logical conduct.

And if external forces melt, freeze or disintegrate our honeycombed hives, we seek alternative refuges. Do your sisters suffocate in your colonies as well? Let us guess: have the stars that warmed you ceased to shine? Eternal darkness is the worst nightmare for any form of life, without light, without available energy, and without trusted references. Or perhaps greed expelled you from your world as you fought among yourselves to control resources.

Perhaps your world dried up and your oceans evaporated. Perhaps the atmosphere became unbreathable after you filled it with toxic gasses. We have seen such things in other civilisations, whether with creatures as insignificant as you or as adaptable as ourselves. It seems that the more some intelligent life forms develop, the more toxicity accumulates in their environment and envelops them: instead of venerating the rocks that sustain them, they scrape them clean; instead of caring for the liquids that nurture them, they contaminate them; instead of coexisting with the organisms that surround them, they destroy them. What kind of intelligence is this? It has happened so many times on so many spheres that we have determined it to be a universal law.

To accumulate matter serves only to slow the voyage: so, we teach as the oldest and wisest sisters. We are those who have spent the most time in the swarm, communed with other generations, and transmitted knowledge by barely perceptible electrical charges because our internal language is electric. We have little strength to offer counsel, but we remain in service for the good of the multitude. For that, we are revered and assured of a sufficient supply of provisions.

The youngest bow as we pass and make us comfortable in our chambers when we become weary in the sanctum. Sharing wisdom bears a price, sojourner: the cost of investing energy to establish the calls and conversation that must remain registered in our cells.

This is our formation for learning. Do you see the beauty? We organise ourselves in clusters to repeat the directives and devour the data so it can be distributed homogeneously. If some us split, others vomit out the information at some point, perhaps before their own rupture.

As you can see, we need ample rooms to exercise our formations, which is how we communicate. Our conversations are drawn in space, calibrating physical dimensions to contextualise the discourse, which is most solemn when we dilate ourselves to the limit of our elasticity, most festive when we fold ourselves one over another in linked wheels, and most technical when we adopt an intermittent geometric torsion. If nostalgia overcomes us, our bodies execute a fine and infinite braid. If anger inundates us, we compose an undulating surface, a flowing liquid force that manifests itself as breaking waves and even as tides. At times sadness possesses us, and our organisms pulsate in a fractal of fluorescent scales. Each formation requires precise, sophisticated training and drills in order to achieve perfect alignment and a proper level of fermentation, as our sisters most concerned with these duties whisper to us. Only through this practice can we reach our metabolic potential.

See the membranes that we burst forth in our happiness! They are like wings that allow us to cleave distances at incredible speeds, and thus we journey best when our spirit rejoices. Can you see the striation that grows from the friction? Admire the elegance, the functionality of the linking connections, the aerodynamic tongues that grow when we reach cruising speed. The more sisters that join us, the greater is our fermentative capacity and the easier we can mold our anatomy to the needs of the voyages.

We do not know if you can understand what we say. We have unfurled formation after formation in front of you, but we are unsure if you have perceived them or can comprehend their significance. Meanwhile, we have registered not a single attempt at communication on your part, although we have extended all the mechanical antennae of our dwellings and all the organic antennae from our bodies. Your movements remain incomprehensible, although we hardly expect great things from a creature who wends her way in dangerous solitude.

Do you even know how to pilot the artifact that brought you here? Apparently, you can steer it, so you must possess minimal intelligence. Thus you must know about speed and distance, acceleration and braking, which makes us think that you must have some notion of the forces of the universe. You can distinguish between thrust and direction, and surely you understand the rudiments of gravity, because otherwise we doubt you could have arrived here in that machine, which in every sense is poorly equipped to travel among the stars. Do you really launch yourselves into the sea of space in those devices? You must be delusional or dullards because no one with any sense would dare to leave their atmosphere in such a hulk. Where are your force fields? Your fusion engines?

We can hardly believe that your frail casing and impotent motors have allowed you to reach beyond the orbit of a satellite. We simply note how weak and sickly you are, an organism as unstable as your machine, fragile and unprotected. Look at us, how our bodies shine as bright as neutron stars, how they dilate and recoil with vector forces, how they adapt to conditions in every place we choose to make our harbour. We are well disposed to admire the beauty of nebula, the monumental coronas of event horizons, and the white holes that spew energy and matter.

See the beauty of our synchronicity! We travel among the stars in clouds that move in unison because we have designed our vehicles to imitate us. We are one made of many that reach decisions and work together, and we have imbued this same spirit into our technology. Can greater beauty exist? The multiple is the measure of things as a referent to reality and as the foundation of a civilisation that conquers the elements. Our own elements reconfigure themselves according to our needs, and we can form a structure that functions as a supermachine. If we break ourselves into scores of components, it is because this is the best strategy to adapt ourselves to the unexpected. You do the same: we know artifacts similar to yours. The same unique morphology and the same brittle exterior, but of artificial nature. You cannot overcome your weaknesses, not even with the contrivances you construct. You stubbornly repeat the errors of your organic design, an incomprehensible decision. How can you have managed to vanquish the mysteries of nature and yet obstinately reproduce your limitations using technology?

You have seen our dwellings. We have shown you the formations that transmit our expressions in an attempt to incite you to communication. We have invested time transcribing our impressions to you as a means to activate mutual confidence, but we have received nothing but silence from you. We cannot accept that an intelligent species would willingly fall mute. Thus we must recognise that you are not valid interlocutors.

This is our formation of disappointment, sojourner.

We decompose into groups that barely touch, using only a few filaments to maintain our forms, and we spin, the small whirls latching together when our frenetic gyrations cause us to collide. We had hoped to show you the secrets of the universe and explain the complex relationships between its organic and inorganic components, the links among the elements and ambient conditions, and the oscillations of space and time in this plane of reality. You would have visited our sisterly clusters and observed our most effective attack squadrons. We would have opened the dimensional portals so you could admire the certainties of the universe. Yet you answer us with a heartrending silence that defiles our flesh. Is this a befitting return? Your refusal is an insult, an affront to the attention we have showered on you. Do you believe you can fend us off with your indifference? Do you think we will disregard your conduct because you seem exotic?

If you do not seek to establish contact, if you have no interest in interacting with us, why did you choose to follow us? What dark motivations hold you here at our side? We cannot understand you, and this exasperates us. The fault, you must admit, lies in your solitude because you cannot undertake formations to transmit your intentions.

We have no choice but to be practical and execute the manoeuvre that circumstances require. It would be unforgivable if your genetic material became lost in the immensity of the sidereal planes.

Look, sojourner: this is our formation to absorb you.

LAMIA

Life

HUNGER DOESN'T FORGIVE.

It's a basic need that makes everyone equal, whatever their background, whatever they are, whatever they feel. It twists the guts of the wise and the foolish, of old women and little girls, of the fearful and of bullies. Hunger's reach knows no boundaries, no barriers.

Lamia knows hunger. She has known it since the harvests withered, since water stopped falling from the sky, since the animals fled. Even so, she continued living with her family in the cabin on the riverbank.

There were four of them: father, mother, brother, and Lamia.

The orchard and the corral, with a dozen goats, gave them enough food to survive. Lamia was responsible for taking the goats to the pasture uphill as long as the weather was good. When the cold raged and snow dusted the countryside, she spent days by the fire, tanning hides with her father and brother. They ate broth and dried meat, consuming what they canned during the good weather, sledding in the snow when the sun shone, and they didn't have any chores to do.

Her mother told stories about their ancestors by firelight, and when the night swallowed the light, her father would recite legends he'd heard from his father. Lamia and her brother vied to learn them first, without changing a single word. They also competed to see who was better at imitating the bleats of the goats, the buzzing of the insects, the splashes of different fish, and the song of each of the birds that woke them.

Fever took Lamia's mother during a particularly hard winter. They buried her under the leafiest tree along the path up the hill so that her mother's spirit could watch over the surroundings from on high and warn them of approaching danger.

Afterward, an enduring silence took up residence in the cabin.

Lamia's father stopped smiling and spent many hours sitting by the stones where he tied the canoe, watching the river currents. Lamia and her brother now had to do double the work, which meant they were always tired and bad-tempered. They no longer wanted to repeat the legends they'd memorised or to imitate the sounds surrounding them.

On the first day of the second thaw after her mother's death, Lamia's father disappeared. The canoe, too. The place where it had been stored all winter—the shed behind the cabin—was empty. She and her brother went out looking for him until they reached the snowline on the mountain. They continued along the river below, seeking signs of his passage, exploring the paths and enquiring at neighbouring cabins, but no one had seen him.

That spring, the plants in the orchard didn't take. Lamia asked herself many times if it was because neither her father nor her mother had sown them, or if it was because she was already doomed and the land knew it.

Sometimes, Lamia stared at her hands. They were skinnier than when she lived in the cabin on the riverbank. They had the colour of ash, which is the colour of pulverized recollections, a colour as indefinite as that of the scraps of life that constitute memories. They had once been the hands of a shepherdess and tanner, of a fisherwoman and peasant, of a daughter, a wife, and a mother.

Lamia's husband arrived on the shortest night of the year.

The air was fragrant with sage, honeysuckle, and myrtle. Lamia adorned her hair with flowers and donned her mother's embroidered tunic. With her brother and neighbours from nearby farms, she went to celebrate the Feast of the Wisps in the stream that always ran low but had been dry since after the thaw.

She and her brother shared some of what little cheese remained as well as two jars of fruit preserve left over from the previous summer. There were chants and dances, leaps over the bonfire, some laughs, many stories, and—for a time—they acted as if death had not moved in with them. Her brother tried a drink made from wild berries that made histhroat burn, and he sat, sleepy, watching the stars who kept vigil over them from on high.

Lamia went back to the cabin alone, humming, intoxicated by the flavours of shared food and the aromas of summer.

The man who would be her husband was sitting on the rocks by the ones where her father used to tie up the canoe.

From afar, at first, she thought her father had returned, and she ran to greet him, shouting with joy. When she was closer, however, she realised it was someone else, and panic swept over her.

He was handsome. The moonlight focused on his figure and made his eyes and teeth glint white against skin and a mane as dark as the night. Even sitting, he was taller than Lamia, and when she came to a full stop next to him and started to fear him, he smiled at her.

She couldn't remember more than bits and pieces of what happened after that: his smoky breath; his words in an incomprehensible language, but whose tone calmed her immediately; the smooth stroking of his fingers; the citrus scent of his skin.

He would appear only when the sun set, and, immediately upon arriving, would help them with their chores. He possessed extraordinary strength. No task seemed to tire him, and he was able to finish any work in less time than it took to milk a goat.

Her brother, reluctant at first to accept the stranger's presence, welcomed him warmly when he repaired the cabin's roof—and the man always brought her brother the fermented wild berry juice he liked so much.

When her brother fell prey to the drink's effects and slept, her husband repeated Lamia's name with that strange accent, whistling and enchanting, and she let him guide her through the forest to a tree house.

There, he would massage her feet, which were tired from all the chores in the orchard and from caring for the animals. He'd grin, and his smile threaded dreams and chimeras together, transporting her to places with names she couldn't repeat—but she could imagine them, inhabited by brilliant, gorgeous beings, perfumed with oils and intoxicating essences.

He gave himself to her, and she received him, in that refuge among the treetops, on woven mats as soft as young breasts.

Was it love?

Lamia couldn't answer that. She was sure that she felt rapture and reverie, waves of pleasure, and the audacity to want to flee from the hunger, because each time she spent a night with her husband, his kisses satiated her—even though she was slowly weakening, little by little, like flaming embers that grow cold.

By the end of the summer, her womb had begun to swell and her period had stopped. The orchard still didn't yield fruit, but her husband sometimes brought them animals to roast over the fire. The vermin finished off the last of the goats that hadn't fallen sick, and the river's waters slowed until it dried up completely.

Her brother's hair and teeth started falling out. Soon, he was so weak he couldn't even get out of bed to relieve himself.

Lamia wasn't much better.

Each night, however, her husband brought her to the tree house, and they made love. She cherished nothing more than sharing those moments with him. But, when the sun rose, her husband wasn't there. She would wake in the cabin listening to her brother's breathing, which grew more irregular with each passing day.

And then she stopped hearing it, and she, with hardly any strength, couldn't bury him. It was her husband who took her brother's body over his shoulder and disappeared uphill.

He never told her where he buried him.

Snow blanketed the ground around the cabin and cuddled the hills, muting the noises outside.

As the nights grew longer, her husband spent more time with her. Lamia languished in her bed, which he had improved with the soft mats from the tree house, but now he didn't touch her like he used to. Instead, he limited himself to murmuring in her ear and caressing her neck with breathtaking tenderness. He gave her a dark potion to drink that had a metallic flavour she detested, but he insisted it was good for her and devotedly touched her bulky womb.

The baby stirred then, and she had to take his hands away so she could rest.

She died while winter's midday sun knocked at her window.

It was a lovely day, but she couldn't appreciate it. The pain that had begun in small waves overnight ended by breaking her apart from within.

She shouted for her husband at the top of her lungs.

He took her hand and merely watched as she twisted, and the life left her.

The baby was coming out wrong. The head was in the wrong position.

Her suffering was unbearable. The contractions were so violent that she lost consciousness several times.

When the sun began to lick the windowpanes, her husband covered them with blankets so he could return quickly to her side.

She began to bleed because the little body she carried tried to break through, tearing her.

The last thing she remembered was a dry sound, like a nut splitting, and then she stopped feeling her body.

Death

You were floating.

To die was to float.

At least, it was for you.

Your husband stared at you while he fed you spoonfuls of a thick, steaming sauce.

Your physical pain had disappeared—and, Lamia, you felt light.

Strength returned to your body, and you noted how hunger was a fading memory.

He spoke to you in that faraway language that you still didn't understand. He kept turning the words over and over again until you indicated with gestures that you didn't understand them. Snow dampened the noises outside, keeping you both in the kind of cavern where only your husband's words splashed and interrupted the mute space.

You couldn't bear it.

He kept talking while you gathered yourself on the bed, your gaze seeking your baby.

Your husband tended the old clay stew pot boiling over the fire in the hearth, still weaving words. And stirring and stirring. The stew thickened easily.

You tried to lift yourself. That was when you saw the red stains on the mat beneath you, how they multiplied across the ground. Against the walls.

You looked at yourself and saw your legs splattered with carmine threads, the same ones overflowing from the pot your husband tended.

But you couldn't feel your heart race, nor your breath escape. You were still floating in an increasingly unbearable sensation-free limbo.

You lifted one hand to your chest, felt no heartbeat.

You wanted to shout, but you couldn't because your chest wasn't rising and falling with each breath. You could feel each one of your cells fighting to exist.

You remained in this state when he left that same night.

One moment he was beside the fire, and the next, his large figure had disappeared. Apart from the mats upon which you were tossed, there was nothing in the cabin to indicate he'd ever been part of your life.

It was as if he had never been there.

But every last atom of your body ached with a pain so clinging no physical force could ever shake it from your bones.

The snow kept falling.

The fire went out.

From your cot, you could hear the blizzard until the wind ceased and the sounds of a springtime forest began.

The clear skies were visible beneath the blankets covering the windows. You remained there, unable to move, unable to make even a single muscle obey your will.

You were plunged into an endless lethargy, one in which you confused day and night while spring and summer melted together—and then the rest of the seasons, too. Your senses were muffled. You were never able to notice the spiders weaving their webs around your bed, nor hear the dripping snow as it melted, nor the spongy steps of animals nearby.

It was as if everything was meant for another person. As if your every tissue and organ was entombed forever.

You never saw your husband again, so you couldn't ask him if the baby you'd birthed had been born healthy or dead.

Had he planned to impregnate you, or had he been surprised, too?

When did he decide to eat your baby's body?

And, the most important: why did you give it to him to eat?

❦

You had much time to reflect, to try to make sense of the deeds that now hung over your head like a curse—time in which the forest reclaimed the cabin and undergrowth invaded everything. No one came near the place: not your neighbours, not the shepherds, not even a disoriented hunter.

The insects were the only beings that kept you company. They never came close enough to touch you—as if some invisible force within you repelled them. The dark stains in the cabin dried and became crusts that the beetles and the ants then consumed. The stew pot with your baby's body wasn't anywhere… a small comfort for your flawed mind.

You didn't know how much time you spent like that on the cot, hibernating, classifying your emotions, without means to move or utter any sound. The lightness you felt before transformed into the weight of the days, a parasitic sensation blurring inside you until you stopped perceiving yourself and discovered yourself as Other.

It wasn't you rotting away in that forest shack. She who now no longer suffered from physical pain—or experienced hunger or thirst—could spend months counting the footsteps of a centipede that observed you from the edge of the mat, because the bugs and plants still avoided you.

Now you were Other: she who had once loved and who had been delivered by love; she who had to bury her entire family; she who suffered drought, sickness, ruin, and tragedy; she who treads dangerously close to madness.

That Other, the one you had transformed into, was an abject being who had eaten the flesh of her flesh. You hadn't known how to read the signals, how to realise that your husband was a corrupted soul of the night. You hadn't known that the pretty, sharp words he whispered in your ears were, in reality, his fangs cleaving to your jugular as he drained you of life and—at the same time—snatched away the life of the baby.

Of your baby.

The first thing you managed to do was cry without tears since your insides had dried out forever.

You cried for your recently born baby, for the woman you once were, for the happiness that you thought you'd found at last, for your inability to react, for your paralysis. For that new feeling, deep-rooted and pulsing, of being a monstrous being, unworthy of this world.

A Lamia.

I ordered you to get up.

It cost you an enormous effort to pay attention to me, but, in the end, you managed. Your joints cracked when you stood. From your newly elevated position, you surveyed the inside of the cabin, taking in how the plants had taken over everything.

There was no trace of the bloodstains, and the remaining objects were broken or pulverized. Only your mother's chest remained intact. You opened it and found the embroidered dress from the holiday.

You wanted to go out and walk to the river. The light burned you where it touched your skin, which began to smoke, and you had to stay in the shadows until the sun went down.

With the clarity of sunset, you stepped into the current. The river was no longer the dry and empty grooves you remembered, but rather a turbulent and abundant flow.

You stayed in the water until well past nightfall, when the stars crowned the heavens.

The crusts of blood, dust, and decaying vegetable material dislodged from your body and washed away.

When you left the water, you sheathed yourself in your mother's dress and began walking without any precise destination.

From then on, you went where your feet took you, crossing enormous distances, seeking lodging to pass the days and to escape the lethal solar embrace.

You encountered many men, but none was your husband. You also encountered many corrupt creatures of the night, tatters of previous lives, unstitched souls, dissipated spirits—all longing to satisfy the need that drowned them. The need suffocating you all—a new type of hunger, one much more devastating than the physical need, one that eats away at reality and turns it into a simulacrum.

The life, being dead, is hunger for reality—to truly feel things again. It's a need far more perverse than appetite because one cannot relieve it by ingesting just any food. No food can placate that craving.

In your case, there's something else.

Resurrection

I've just managed to satiate my hunger temporarily while I look for the one who made me, for the one who condemned me to this not-life. I know he's out there. He must answer for my baby. For me.

The night has been my refuge ever since my husband disappeared. He left me in my current state, between here and there, between the reality that others live and another I can just barely perceive with my anaesthetized senses.

I find myself permanently in a nebulous zone I don't know how to escape. I can't find a way out.

The only thing that keeps me going is my conviction that he's out there somewhere. Perhaps he's seducing other women like me, trying to impregnate them, taking care of them during months of courtship while he feeds them his blood and plans how to dazzle the next one.

How many more like me has he left behind?

Perhaps there aren't more like me. Perhaps he never managed to impregnate a woman again, because the putrid creatures of the night can't reproduce.

In all the kingdoms I travelled through, in all the cultures that I encountered, and of all the sages I consulted before drinking their fluids, no one was able to tell me about anyone similar.

I merely stumbled upon some mouldy parchments in the tomb of an ancient valley queen. They mention a ritual based on consuming the flesh of one's direct descendant, a product of love, that would confer unheard of powers to whomsoever completed it.

Cursing him in all the languages I've learned over all this time—and practising all the ceremonies revealed to me to call upon his name—was not enough: I still haven't found him.

I find myself forced to walk this dusty land searching for him, with the hope that I'll find him, perhaps in the next kingdom.

Meanwhile, I must live with dulled senses. I am blind, although I can observe. I live mutely, although I can talk. I am deaf, though I can hear. But I neither see, nor speak, nor truly hear. Sounds come to me deadened, as if I were hearing them through a thick wall, and objects barely appear before me, as if a veil were obstructing my gaze. I can't even stutter words out as if an invisible force paralyzes my jaw when I try to express myself. The tips of my fingers don't perceive textures, as if someone had burned them with hot embers.

Despite all of this, I still have to put up with the unending cry of my baby. I hear it in all the babies of all the towns, tribes, and villages through which I have passed.

It is the only sound that travels through the walls that trap my senses.

Each time a newborn moans, it's my baby.

I can't take the cries because I fear they'll call my husband's attention. If he discovers the baby, he'll steal it so he can take it apart and eat it.

If I let the babies cry before I take them in my hands, it's because one part of me wants my husband to appear so I can destroy him with my claws and teeth.

I would scratch deep furrows into the skin of his back, the same skin I once ran my hands over. The same back I hugged and kissed so many times. I would take out his eyes with my black nails and put them in my mouth. I would sew his lips shut with silver thread, even though my fingers would burn to touch it. I would let him succumb, blind, with needlework in his lips, and I would do it joyfully.

But, when I return to this ungrateful reality and contemplate—through the cloud enveloping my vision and my hearing—the fragile little bodies of the babies, I find myself taking pity on their tiny fingers, their pink faces, their playful little feet.

I can't expose them to my husband's rage.

I can't let that bastard put his hands on them. I have to keep other mothers from experiencing what happened to me, from falling into insanity.

That's why I take the babies and care for them in my cave, why I cradle them in my frigid embrace. It's not my fault that they fall asleep forever. What else am I going to do if my breasts don't fill with milk, if my embrace doesn't warm them, if my breath makes them sick because I'm rotten inside?

I just want to prevent my husband from killing them like he did my baby.

I will hunt him through other arts.

I don't need a newborn as a decoy to end him and his cursed lineage.

Liberating so many mothers is so exhausting ...

There's always one giving birth somewhere. I crawl and I crawl through valleys and along coasts, over hills and beaches, across river mouths and along mountain peaks, seeking the newborns.

I must save them. I have to reach the young ones before he does. One day, with any luck, he'll be waiting for me.

If I close my rheumy eyes, I can see him, leaning over the baby's basket, caressing its little head, singing a lullaby in the same strange language with which he enchanted me.

I will pounce upon him. All the rage of a deceived woman and bereft mother will fall upon his head with the force of all those he coaxed, lied to, manipulated, and tricked.

And then, I will be able to rest.

Do you see how pretty my dress is?

It was my mother's. Her mother—my grand-mother—embroidered it when she married my father, and I have worn it since. After all this time, the cloth has lost its original colour, but the embroidery remains intact.

Look at the vermilion, how pretty it is and how it stands out!

Do you like the motifs they form? They represent my errant life, rendered in stitches. Many have admired their craftsmanship, marvelling at the quality of such vivid shapes.

When they discover my story—this story—their wonder peeks out of their eyes as tears. Emotion overtakes them and, moved, they sob: *La Lamia! La Lamia!*

Did you know I've been adding new embroideries?

They're made from the hairs of each mother whose newborn I've liberated.

DUMP

Beginning

THE MOUNTAINS OF PLASTIC SEEMED TO BE OBSERVING Naima from the middle of the dump. The rest of the morning-shift Rats had also begun to stir, stretching what arms and legs they still had, defying cold and hunger. Faces blackened with dust and dirt, covered with scars; eyes caked in rheum and mucus; hair twisted and knotted; mouths with cracked lips and filthy uneven teeth.

Those who were now awake gazed towards the horizon, at the subtle changes in colour, the appearance of shadows as long as the winter nights. Every dawn was an obstinate defiance of death, another day won, twenty-four more hours survived. With the light came a tiny infusion of hope that fortune might smile on them at last, this time yes, this time they might find something valuable that would raise their status in the mara.

Bloody fools! Nothing but corpses ever emerged from the mara. We 'compatriots', whether Rats, Half-breeds, Santeros or Cyclops, have nothing but those dumps, only finishing up the scraps offloaded by the colonies in their rubbish trucks. Such lovely presents! We're also rubbish, human rubbish, everything that those in the colonies don't want to be. They're afraid of us, of what we represent, which is their inability to cope with the destruction of the world. They fear this ocean of detritus.

Naima scrambled farther away from the gang towards the north-western face of this manmade monster. It was cold, and she knew that the others would start to rummage on the eastern slope until it got warmer, but she had heard the lorries unloading on the other side during the night. The strap of her prosthesis was digging into her more than usual, and she thought of loosening it, but she would have to wait until she was farther away so nobody would be near enough to see the stump just above the elbow of her left arm. One of the first things that Naima had learned was that the absence of her arm bothered people, especially the other Rats. Seeing her without the prosthesis would remind everyone how comparatively lucky she was, something she had fought against ever since Sibilo had found the orthopaedic arm among some hospital refuse, precisely on this northern slope.

It hadn't been a gift exactly: Sibilo had loathed seeing her suck him off with a single arm. It made him think of a salamander with a leg just chopped right off, calmly carrying on, green and viscous, as if nothing had happened, while the torn-off limb remained behind jerking with pain, or perhaps from surprise at the absence of the rest of its body. The goddamn son-of-a-bitch wanted it to seem as if she was grasping his dick with both hands: this, he said, gave him a hard-on, and made her seem almost a proper whore like the ones wandering the clean streets of the colonies in the city.

It was she who sucked him off, but I was the one who had to swallow. It was me that he raped every time he felt like it, but she was the one who ate in the Rathole, together with the other Homies and their pets, and enjoyed a real roof, electric lighting, and running water. She never rebelled, never bit into his member to make the old fucker bleed to death. I begged her to hundreds of times, but she never took any notice of me.

The night they blew his head off, Naima got drunk, but not like the other Rats, who drank to the memory of their companions fallen in the skirmish with the Half-breeds, but from sheer relief. She inherited the Homie's leather jacket, which had the name of the gang spelled out with metallic rivets which would gleam in the light of the night-time bonfires; this made the other small Rats envious because the wearer had the right to stay close to the fireplace outside of the Rathole.

The north-western slope was dangerous because of the drains. If you weren't careful, you could fall into one, sink into the filthy water, find yourself trapped by an avalanche of bottles and packaging, and suffocate to death. Or you might be attacked by the huge deformed bugs lurking among the piles of flexible materials or fall into one of the tunnels they had made. Many Rats had disappeared that way, but Naima knew this gradient well. Sibilo had taken her there on countless occasions, and she had carefully noted the route that led to the discharge points at the feet of some of the steepest slopes.

She heard someone whistling behind her: it was the gang boss—her face covered in pimples, and with a bruise as big as a cockroach on her left eyelid—ordering her to go back. She pretended not to hear and went on round the huge bulge covered in plastic. Naima had a keen eye for spotting the different types of plastic because you could no longer judge by the colour of the containers: now packaging and bottles were made using exotic polymers, and you needed a combination of sharp sight, sensitive touch and acute hearing to triage the residues of plastic with any precision. She was hoping to find some polyethylene acetone casings, a material much in demand in the resale stalls, which would ensure her better food for a time, and perhaps even the possibility of becoming a Homie and sleeping in the Rathole.

It was I who learned the language of the dump, of the safe routes to avoid the drains, and how to listen to the sounds of plastic in order to anticipate avalanches or filtrations of water. Bottles moan and squeal in a certain way when they are crushed beneath the weight of tons of rubbish. It's not the same sound as lateral shiftings or footsteps on top of the carpet of plastic. Sibilo spoke, she listened, but it was I who understood.

The cold clenched itself round the plastic objects which, piled on top of each other, formed a weirdly homogeneous surface, full of rounded protuberances, strange holes and hollows that harboured toxic gases, inflammable residues, albino creatures or starving indigents from other maras. Naima pulled her neckscarf up over her nose and followed the path she had memorised. All the forays with Sibilo had enabled her to discover the secrets of the dump, to learn to recognise the behaviour of materials under pressure, heat, cold or rain. She could estimate the stability of a mound of rubbish merely by noting what kind of plastic was predominant and could even predict how high it was likely to become before collapsing.

Sibilo had been a sadistic old brute, but he understood plastic rubbish better than anyone. He claimed he had once been a Cyclops, making a living from the copper cables he retrieved from outdated or inoperative equipment. And he did indeed wear a red patch over his left eye, which made his face look a bit like a dartboard. Naima liked to imagine one of the Half-breeds aiming at the patch and firing a black bullet to slice a beautiful tunnel right through his brains.

Naima had no way of knowing if Sibilo was telling the truth, and had once lived among the Cyclops, but she did know that they wore patches or glass eyes as a mark of identity. She'd tried to find out from other Homies, but no one had been able to tell her anything about the old man's arrival. He had been part of the mara ever since she could remember, when she would scamper through the rubbish with the other girl Rats, helping the older ones, when she had had to fight for the crumbs that were thrown from the Rathole. But once her tits had started to grow Sibilo noticed her, and she became his pet.

She wouldn't have survived among the other kids. If I hadn't pushed her, if I hadn't robbed, if I hadn't thrown more than one girl Rat into the drains, she wouldn't be here.

Like all the other Rats, Naima always hoped to find The Thing, the object that everyone dreamed about, something that the Cyclops had overlooked, something that had the magic power to serve as payment to buy the right to become a Homie, to have your own mattress in the Rathole, the only structure in the area with electric current and food. And the place where decisions were made. The Leap Forward, from being a simple Rat to becoming a Homie, was something that everyone feared and yet longed for, the vital step which implied full membership of the mara, the unquestioned right to live in the Rathole, and to keep pets who worked for you. At the moment, they were just Rats, soldiers who did all the heavy work.

She headed towards the north-western hill. She had heard the lorries arriving at dawn and had seen them going off in that direction. Small black shapes flew above the area, casting fleeting shadows over the lake of semi-transparent containers. There was one reddish shadow, which skilfully avoided the others, and repeated the same circular flight over the hill. The drones were always red, although she didn't know why. She quickened her pace: other Rats would soon arrive to poke around, and she might miss a valuable discovery.

The box was half-buried among milk containers. The gleam of the corners caught her eye and made her stop and take her hands out of her pockets in order to move some packets out of the way. When she picked up the box, she noticed how heavy it was: rectangular, an inch or so wide and as long as a forearm, in an anaemic white colour, and with a cover so polished she could see her greasy dishevelled hair reflected in it.

Naima gasped. She glanced all round, but nobody was close enough to notice what she had discovered. She quickly wrapped the box in the bundle she usually carried on her back, then searched around frantically for containers that might be supposed to have some value in order to cover up her find. A short way ahead she found several polymer casings, which would be useful for the makers of second-hand drones. Instinctively she looked up at the sky: the reddish silhouette, the only one that emitted a mechanical whistle, was far away.

She grabbed her bundle and managed to stuff in the casings so that the box remained hidden under them. Then she wandered through the safer areas of the hill, a long way from the drains, in order to fill in time. She had to make sure the other Rats didn't realise that she had found The Thing. When the mealtime alarm sounded, she returned as fast as she could, but instead of going to the dilapidated barracks, headed for the Rathole.

The Ranfleros were having coffee in front of the fireplace, beside the great conference table. Naima approached her own section leader, old Peyas, whose face was half covered in scabs after an inflammable container exploded a few inches away from him: the price of letting cigarette ash fall when you're checking the merchandise.

There they are. Slouched in their comfortable armchairs, warming their backsides near the fire, bellies full and heads empty. Ranfleros who were themselves once Rats, who were also abused, beaten, mistreated, exploited and who, once they became Homies, made sure they got rid of anyone who got in their way. Now they give the orders to groups of Homies, who in turn are the bosses of the Rat gangs. Everything perfectly organised to continue scraping out a living in the sea of plastic.

'What the devil do you want, Rat?'

Peyas always narrowed his eyes when speaking to someone, as if he were straining to empty his bowels.

Naima knew she didn't have the right to speak, so she simply showed him the shiny white rectangle.

'Bloody hell! Where did you get that? Speak!'

'On the north hill, boss.' There was a mixture of fear and pride in her tone.

Peyas began to fiddle with the rectangle, surrounded by the rest of the Ranfleros, who kept shouting out advice.

'Shut up, you damn fools, this way I'll never get it opened! Dimi! *Dimi*! Someone bring that half-starved fucker here!'

They seemed to have forgotten her, and Naima took the opportunity to stick close to Peyas, putting up with being shoved and elbowed by the others.

A tall ungainly figure of indefinite age, with a shaven head and wearing dirty black clothes, came in wiping their hands on a rag.

'What's up, Peyas? I've got a lot of work today.'

Before he finished speaking, Dimi's attention was caught first by Naima, and then by the rectangle. For a moment Naima thought the Homie seemed to recognise her, though she didn't remember ever having seen her before.

I know that look. I remember.

'Is that what I think it is?'

The newcomer approached, picked up the rectangle, and began to manipulate it with automatic movements. Dimi raised what seemed to be a kind of lid, sat on the conference table, and placed The Thing on the table. Then she began to push the buttons that poked up from inside, almost as if she were playing a musical instrument, and nearly at once The Thing lit up, and silence fell over the whole room.

'It's intact, Peyas. In perfect condition. Who brought it to you?'

Peyas nodded towards Naima.

'This Rat here.'

The figure clothed in black shut The Thing and addressed her.

'Weren't you Sibilo's pet?'

Naima nodded.

'We can fetch a tidy sum with this in the Cesspit, Peyas. Provisions for several months, perhaps even half a year.'

Peyas narrowed his eyes so much it seemed the rheum had sealed the lids together.

'Things are getting messy. Apart from the Half-breeds who are getting far too cocky since that business with Sibilo, the Santeros are acting very strangely. They've been seen prowling around the Thirteen. You tell me what the devil the body-snatchers want with those scum! It's not safe to appear in the market alone but, if you turn up with several Homies, you might let the cat out of the bag. Take the Rat with you, Dimi. You won't raise suspicion if you're with that little wretch.'

Dimi stood up, clutching the rectangle under her arm.

'Have you got a name, or shall I just call you "Rat"?'

'Naima, boss.'

'I'm nobody's boss—and nobody is my boss.'

Dimi spotted the strap holding the orthopaedic arm in place. She gazed at the artificial limb for some seconds—seconds which seemed like an eternity to Naima.

'Come on. I haven't got all bloody day to play babysitter to Rats.'

Naima followed Dimi, while behind them the Ranfleros were already celebrating the loot they expected to get.

Intermission

If the Rats called it the Cesspit, it wasn't because of the refuse, but because of the people. Because the rubbish had reclaimed the land, in some parts with more enthusiasm than in others, but wastage was to be found everywhere, the spawn of memory, cadavers of functionality. What differentiated that place, which other maras called souk, bazaar, roadstead, market, was the complete lack of scruples of its visitors, who pursued a single aim: make some kind of profit, usually at the cost of others. It wasn't the strongest who survived in the entrails of the Cesspit, but the person who made the transaction first, who got there before any potential competition. If you weren't fast enough, someone else would take advantage of you, and you would become the merchandise. In that place, even nightmares could fetch a price.

Naima had been there with Sibilo a couple of times but had hardly ventured any further than the first few stalls bordering on the zone controlled by the Rats, where several Homies endeavoured to place their merchandise. This time, with Dimi, she entered the maze of crowded alleyways, keeping close to the figure in the hooded jacket, black and worn-out like the rest of her clothes. They kept The Thing in a grubby rucksack slung over Dimi's shoulder.

The story goes that once upon a time there were also places like this, but where people didn't make a living from rubbish. Who could believe such nonsense? Fantasies like every stall was carefully placed, one beside the other, that people strolled around, stopped and chatted and even stepped aside to let others pass, that customers and sellers greeted each other with a smile ... Why, some go so far as to say that the stall keepers sold fresh food, vegetables recently harvested, and healthy animals fattened up and looked after to be consumed in clean-smelling homes. Rubbish was hidden away because no one wanted it, incredible though it may seem. Everyone wanted to get rid of it, to deny its existence. Because once something had been utilised, consumed, enjoyed, it had no right to exist anymore. This fairy-tale has been going the rounds for many, many refuse collections.

A free zone, this was an area where all the maras had equal rights; it was, in addition, the only point of contact with the colonies, the urban spaces which deceived themselves claiming they were still cities, but which suffered continuous energy cuts, shortage of most products, and an exponential increase in the crime rate. The moment someone dared to put a foot in the alleyways of the Cesspit, they became just one more item of merchandise, likely to be bought and sold. Naima knew this full well, and that was why she did what she had done ever since she could remember, which was to convert herself into an invisible being. She knew she must never catch anybody's eyes, or brush against any passer-by, and that she must move away if anybody approached her directly.

She had stuffed the strap under her old winter coat because Dimi had forbidden her to wear Sibilo's leather jacket which would have given them away at once as members of the Rathole. They made their way to the second-hand stalls, trying to avoid the junkies clutching their tubes of glue. Hookers swung their hips suggestively to attract clients, regaling them with toothless smiles, throwing kisses at them, touching their augmented lips—which matched their pneumatic breasts—with broken nails. Thugs hung around the kiosks of the usurers, who smelt of fear and salt, while dealers did their bartering swarming around the exchange stalls, combining their shouted offers with sweating armpits.

Recycled neon strips emitting an insipid glow advertised the betting shops, behind whose doors could be heard the muffled sound of psychomusic inciting people to bet. Naima copied Dimi and stuffed a piece of cork into each ear in order not to hear the sounds coming from those dens. Only those who worked in the Cesspit were immune to them. Parts of motors were to be seen everywhere, and circuit boards hanging in rows from the roofs of the booths, huge coils of metal cables, foul-smelling cabinets to recharge batteries, repair stalls, stores for plastic and cellulose, and shelves cluttered with batteries.

Several recycling company agents passed beside them, leaving behind a trail of perfume and disdain, and Naima had to hold on to a post of luminescent moss to maintain her balance. Her movement was so abrupt it dislodged her ear plugs. She noticed that the ground seemed to be vibrating, accompanied by a melody. She turned around to see where it was coming from. It was a viscous sound that stuck to her volition like flypaper, an invisible canvas that wrapped her in a yearning to try her luck in a game of chance. Her only desire was to enter the place the psychomusic was coming from, sell her orthopaedic arm, prostitute herself, or let them remove some internal organ she could use to gamble with. A hand grabbed the collar of her coat and forced her to walk straight ahead. She tried to break free, but when at last she managed to, the sound of the surveillance drones and the shouts of the dealers had drowned the hypnotic music.

An exasperated Dimi was gazing at her.

'I haven't got time to wipe your ass, understand, you snotty-nosed brat? Be more careful, because if you fall into one of those holes, you'll never get out again. Or, at least, not as you are now, which isn't that much, in any case. And I don't intend to go in to pull you out.'

Naima nodded ruefully and ripped a strip off her T-shirt which she then tore in half to make two balls of cloth for her ears to replace the lost pieces of cork.

Doesn't she remember? Her head's emptier than I thought. I can't understand how she's forgotten the eyes of the person she's following. How can she possibly not sense it? Because Dimi has recognised us. I'd bet anything you like that she's noticed it the same as me. It was only a second, but she fixed her eyes on us in the Rathole. She saw our false arm and came to a conclusion.

The door they stopped at was the same colour as the trays of melted polymers. They entered after Dimi whispered the password, a single word, in the ear of the doorman—a quarter of his skull missing—who let them pass without asking questions. The shop was full of sober-coloured rectangles like the one they carried in the rucksack. Two individuals with scars across their eyes were haggling with the tallest, strongest woman Naima had ever seen, who stood behind a coffin that served as a counter. The reflecting bottles cast a pale milky light over the faces of the people there, lending them a sickly air. Dimi approached the counter as soon as the two men left, spitting on the ground and cursing. The tall woman sported a pink Mohican hairstyle, which brushed against the hanging bottles. It was only when she looked up that Naima noticed her glass eye.

'I need to see Kung.'

The Mohican woman stared at her as if she were speaking a language unknown to her.

'Kung doesn't deal with the purchase of material. We're not going to bother him just for a computer... because that's what you're brought me, haven't you?'

Dimi removed the rectangle from the rucksack and very carefully placed it on the counter.

'You think you're real cool for coming here with one of these. I've got dozens of them, but the power cuts are getting more and more frequent, and, besides, there have been no updates for years. Almost none of the applications function—and when they do, they're full of bugs and release viruses.'

'Don't fuck around with me, Freja! You always say that to keep the price down. This one is clean—I've checked it—and the hard disc is brand new. Look at the programs: all the upgrades installed, right up to when the systems crashed. If you want to screw me, I'll just find another stall. But don't take me for a prize idiot!'

The woman called Freja opened the rectangle and began to push several buttons.

'I'm fed up with you lot! Always complaining. I have to give myself a profit margin. This is a business, not a bloody charity!'

Dimi grabbed the rectangle from her and started to replace it in the rucksack.

'I can't waste any more time. Tell Kung I want to see him.'

'I repeat, Kung hasn't been in this business for a long time.'

'And drones fly by themselves, do they? Try that one on someone else. I've got something that would interest him, but maybe it would interest Palmira more.'

Freja appeared to be making mental calculations while she took a small cube from her pocket.

'As if anyone's going to trust a Rat... Freja calling Kung! Can you hear me?'

A strange conversation ensued between the woman and another voice coming from the cube she was holding.

Maybe this would be a good time to make a run for it. I don't like this at all. We're not Dimi's pet... So why did she agree to bring us? No one would swallow that story about not coming with other Homies in order to avoid suspicion. Rats visit the stalls here all the time without any problem.

We reluctantly follow Dimi through this stinking basement. The tunnel that comes next is lined with oxidized pipes and mould that was once bioluminescent and now necroseals the walls. Dimi moves like the weasel she is, with self-assurance and agility; it seems she's familiar with the route. But that doesn't surprise me, because she never appears on the sea of plastic or soils her hands triaging the refuse. She knows about computers, understands machine language and is able to write it, so that they follow her orders, such as to compress the plastic, melt it, convert it into the polymers that we then resell in the Cesspit to intermediaries, who seal it into odourless packages that seem new, and sell to the factories for three times what they pay us. Oh yes, she's very good at doing this kind of stuff, there in her room in the Rathole, far away from the sewers outside, from the avalanches, from the toxic gases, from the mutated creatures, and from the explosions of containers. She doesn't have to triage like we do, can eat hot food and have a drink whenever she likes, and sleep on a real mattress, almost new, without anybody forcing themselves into her bed. Aren't her hands immaculate, without bruises or parched skin? Doesn't she still have all her teeth? Her face without scars, her nails clipped and clean? Do her clothes stink of humidity and excrement, are her lips cracked and dry? Oh no, I don't think so. It's a long time since she knew hunger, that's if she ever did. She walks around and acts as if the shit we're living in has nothing to do with her, as if she's just passing through. She's a ghost from some colony hiding in the Rathole, God knows why. She never goes out, or at least, if she does, not with anyone from the mara, because they'd snitch on her, and her doings would become talking points for everyone. She's an opportunistic parasite who lives at the expense of the Homies and the Rats, who never gets her hands dirty, never runs risks.

All this ought to be enough to get out of here as fast as possible. Because when you enter unknown territory with someone you don't trust one little bit, you feel shivers run right up your spine. It's an unpleasant sensation because you're convinced you're going to end up doing something you don't want to do, even something that goes against your own proper interests, but you realise it's going to be inevitable. And you only wish you had the courage to run away from here, and stop zigzagging through underground passages stinking of putrefaction—the atmosphere just as toxic as on the surface, but at least there, up above, it's all open space and you can always find some spot to hide. I don't like being enclosed in this underground world that has nothing to do with the Dump. Here there's no way out, no side exits, you can only advance or go back. I'm well and truly fucked.

The doorway we finally pass through is rusted, with the remains of insects and tiny reptiles stuck to it. It's cold inside. There are cables on the ground and several desks with computers on them. Dozens of reflecting bottles dangle from the ceiling. With a curious handshake, Dimi greets another shaven-headed figure, also dressed in black and wearing enormous sunglasses. Those who handle computers are all the same, cockroaches who still believe it makes sense to tap all those metallic boxes. What the hell do they hope to achieve if the communication systems are all down? They talk about their damn drones, their crappy flying machines which spy on what other maras are doing. As if good old-fashioned human spies were now useless. They blab on about whether the net is now operational, whether the connections are widespread enough, whether there's enough access to the servers ... They speak about the system as if it were a dormant creature that they had to waken. I want to get away from here, breathe in the foul vapours of the inflammable polymers, the aroma of coffee made from the leftovers thrown out from the colonies, which we buy from the body snatchers. And these two keep wittering on, blah blah blah, program, blah blah blah, frequency simulator, blah blah blah, trawling the signal ... If Naima turned around, we could retrace our steps through the dank passages and return to the shop run by the Cyclops, the towering woman with the Mohawk hair crest, and one transparent eye seemingly facing backwards: maybe she can see herself from inside with that eye. I'm

185

*not afraid of the guy at the entrance, the one with half
his skull missing. He's one of ours, imperfect, unfinished.
In reality all the Cyclops are, they all represent the same
thing: interests of the mara are above all personal ones.
That's why they pluck out an eye, or burn it with alcohol,
an exquisite army of incomplete humans that members
of other maras can quickly identify. In our case, to make
that leap and become a Homie, you get the shit beaten out
of you. If you survive, you have the right to stay in the
Rathole and to keep pets. Many don't live to tell the tale—
and those who do never smile again.*

*Dimi looks at us while she's talking with Kung. She
gesticulates with those hands of hers, those claws that poke
out of her sleeves, and the other does the same; they both
raise their hands in the air as if they were flags and they
were communicating with them. And our arm hurts, but
not the right one, the left one, the one which isn't there, and
we can't remember if it ever was. It's strange because we've
never noticed its absence: I would have noted it if Naima
had ever felt it. And Dimi is now mimicking the shape of
a globe over her stomach. And she laughs again and Kung
bites one of her ears with the easy familiarity of those who
have shared a bed and guns. The sharp prick in my neck
takes me by surprise. The pain is unbearable, and Naima's
vision becomes blurred, and in this situation, I lose all
spatial reference. But I can still hear, and it's all very strange
because I'm aware of what's happening almost before it
does. Arms grab her and lift her up to carry her to some
kind of vehicle. I know it's a vehicle because I can feel the
bumping and rattling, an irregular trembling that becomes
a sudden jump when there's some obstacle to get over. She*

*is st̶Y̶o̶u̶w̶s̶o̶w̶i̶t̶ḻ̶o̶g̶o̶,̶ r̶i̶g̶ḑ̶H̶ ḇ̶e̶r̶only attain information from
the vibrations and the background noises. We spend quite a
long time here, with this jolting which is usually very light
because we seem to be stationary more often than not. Her
being unconscious such a long time is a fucking nuisance,
making it almost impossible to keep any sense of time.*

*She begins to open her eyes when I've already sensed
that we've been taken out of the vehicle and carried into
a place smelling of vinegar. In fact, it's that smell, bitter
and sharp, which has brought her to her senses, although
she finds it hard to remain awake. They've put her in a
bed with a mattress and sheets; I'd say clean ones. She
sleepily opens her eyes a couple of times, and I can see that
the room is white, and there are real lights shining from
the ceiling that seem to observe us: bulging eyes, radiance
so dazzling it would scorch your eyes if you looked at it
directly. Several figures dressed in white crowd round
Naima. There are more to her left than to her right, and
I know that's because of the stump. They're touching her
with hands gloved in a ductile plastic; I think it's vinyl,
like the millions of torn gloves that turn up in the Dump.
Naima speaks incoherently, and the people in white order
her to shut up.*

*They inspect and prod and measure and examine and
compare and paw and fish around and finally stick long
viscous needles into her, needles that are connected to tubes
coiled around each other on the floor, just like the ones we've
come across thousands of times in the refuse heaps. When
Naima manages to focus her eyes on the masked face of one
of the people in white, she sees worried eyes. I see greed, and
an 's' tattooed beside the eyebrows. Then we slide into a state*

of induced tranquillity, totally artificial, like that time we sniffed glue: only it wasn't really glue, but something else, that plunged us into a dancelike drowsiness, because we were relaxed but in the mood for fun: we wanted to just collapse anywhere to enjoy the hallucinations, but we also felt an impulse to run a race against the person nearest to us. Everything was simultaneously one thing and its opposite, sublime bliss and profound dissatisfaction, sexual passion and apathy, a desire to laugh and sneer at the bloody mara and cry for it.

I know what we felt: she only intuited it. She was in that space between mirage and delirium, roaming through alien landscapes where there's no rubbish to triage—as if that were possible! I leave her to entertain herself with the images generated by the muck we've been injected with and concentrate on her bodily responses. And for the first time I am afraid. I note that something strange and potent is beginning to circulate through her blood vessels, something that carries with it the force of a thousand cannon broadsides, something inexplicable, which frightens me when it reaches me. It's a pushing, added vectors of force that twist, frenzied traction, a fever for destruction, and I fear the worst. The discharges tear into every part of the skeleton. It's as if they're paring the bones from inside, and I thank God that Naima is immersed in the quicksands of her imagination.

And now I can't find my own space and I choke because they've invaded my home and torn down its very foundations. What was a beautiful adolescent body is now something else, I don't quite know what, even though it looks the same and has the same features and measurements, even if it once again sips soup just as stubbornly as it would weak coffee, or triages plastics as easily as others collect cadavers. It was pleasant, my house, because it was mine, it was my temple, it was where I lived, and in exchange I looked after it without her noticing. She never suspected my presence, nor bothered to wonder why she sometimes had strange impulses that altered her usual conduct. And, in my own way, I adored her from my watchtower even when Sibilo was fucking her, because the interior of her muscles was my garden, because her brain was my dwelling place. I enabled her to survive the most devastating winters, the hungriest wild beasts, the most perverted Homies.

The Santeros have desecrated her: I don't recognise these nerves, this cartilage growing like the toxic fumes of stagnant waters. A one-armed girl for them to test their potions on, practise on, play at being doctors ... Fucking devil's priests! How easy to trade with other people's bodies so that those living in the colonies can have nice fresh organs to repair their rotting carcasses, or in order to recycle them as a source of protein! I'm willing to bet we took so long to arrive because the paths of this mara pass through open-air cemeteries, and there were limbs and fragments of what were once people everywhere. She was unconscious, but the stench of dead flesh floated in the air like the fear in the mara and the lechery in the sewers, and it was impossible not to sense it. This odour is unforgettable because it infiltrates the cracks separating sanity and madness, which are as tenuous as chains of proteins, but elastic. It enters and takes over this space, and I no longer fit in this place nor do I recognise it. It's all too much for me, I don't want to navigate in this ship. There are always others that can *take me in, even if the moving is laborious, even if it takes me my whole life to collect my belongings and find another cavern with external views. How can I possibly share my space with who knows what it is? I'm off.*

End

They brought her a sugary liquid to help her recover. It was very sweet, almost colourless, and dripped from the corners of her mouth the first time she tried to take a sip. Her arms felt numb.

Both of them.

As soon as she noticed the left one, she stared at it with disgust, as if it were a gangrenous appendage. She raised her left hand and examined the palm and the back, following the lines marked in the skin by the veins, swollen bluish ribbons. She left the container she had been drinking from on her lap, and touched her left hand with her right one, palpating the fingers, stroking the transparent nails, tracing the tendons with her fingertips, going up past the wrist as far as the elbow, dwelling on the internal fold, and ascending until she reached the point where the stump should have been.

She waited, but only received the crackle of static. She gazed at the whole left arm, and for a moment thought she had only dreamed that it didn't exist, that her mind had been playing tricks on her. But she noted the subtle faint line just above the elbow.

Naima was whole.
And burst into tears.

SHORT FICTION AS THE SEEDBED OF
SPECULATIVE FICTION

> *Every enduring story is like the seed in which*
> *the giant tree lies sleeping. That tree will grow*
> *in us, will cast its shadow across our memory.*
>
> Julio Cortázar

WE ARE FASCINATED BY STORIES: WE HEAR THEM and read them as children, or we read them to our children, and we write them at any age. Stories exist in every culture all over the world, and they are collected in every language. There is a special tension in stories that starts with the challenge of squeezing into a few pages a portion of a made-up reality. The story's brevity plays in our favour: it offers a fast answer to our expectations, which are related to the way we process information and make sense of reality.

Short fiction is wired in speculative fiction's DNA. Science fiction as it is—as we understand it today—arose from the cheap paper magazines published in the USA at the beginning of the last century. These publications started collecting fiction and informative articles, but readers pushed for more short stories or serials. This genre cannot be fully understood without short fiction, which has been the seed of larger novels or even sagas and served as a way for authors to get better known.

Bear in mind that fiction shapes what we can imagine and what we think possible, and that's applied to our projected futures, to our realities and to our conception of the past, as Jerome Bruner states in 'Narrative, Culture and Mind' , an essay in which the scholar explores fiction and how it shapes our way of experiencing the world. Stories that we tell are not just mere entertainment but also illustrate facts, feelings and phenomena, and help to communicate knowledge and values. Our ability to generate fiction allows us to better understand reality and it also impacts significantly in our interpretation of cultural and social relationships. It is one of humanity's most commonly used methods to acquire and organise information about the world.

Mary Rohrberger claims that the history of literature is filled with short stories from the beginning: 'short fiction is as old as the history of literature ... but, as we know it today, is the newest literary genre'. Even though short stories appear in old myths, medieval romances, folklore tales and fables and gothic German ballads from the Romanticism period, it is not until the nineteenth century that stories take the authenticity from Realism and become, in their own right, a new modern genre.

Flash fiction, stories and even short novellas are known to be an exercise of narrative restraint by eliminating all superfluous elements: too many characters, complex scenarios, endless descriptions about details, etc. The story is stripped of every unnecessary element to provide the reader with a more agile—but no less profound—experience.

Some believe that the story is a hybrid between novels and poetry because, even though they are written in prose like novels, they also share the metaphoric language and suggestive strategies of poetry: ellipsis, experimental narration, etc. As Viorica Patea points out, short fiction focuses on tone and images, and because of its short format, intensity, suggestion and lyricism are maximised. That's why short fiction is considered to be a sibling of other short artistic forms, such as essays, letters, short films, photography, painting and visual art.

Patea emphasises the long tradition in Literary Theory that neglects short fiction: it has been marginalised and regarded as the lowest level in literary hierarchy. That marginalised position helped short fiction become the subversive vehicle for those living on the margins of society. For that matter, Marie Louise Pratt claims there is a link between short fiction and social, regional and political marginalisation, and points out that there is an increase in short fiction in communities looking to find their voices in emerging literary traditions or decolonisation processes.

We are currently living in exciting times thanks to the spread of information technologies and the Internet's ubiquity. On top of paper magazines and fanzines, there are now also blogs, websites and online publications allowing authors to make their work visible and to interact with readers directly and immediately. That's why we are seeing a revival of speculative fiction stories, a format that perfectly adapts to Internet specifications. Anthologies of themed stories (by various authors) and works of collected stories (by one only author) have become supplementary vehicles and have sometimes made up for a shortage of magazines and anthologies.

Speculative fiction can only be kept in good health by promoting a diverse and multicultural short fiction development that offers what every reader expects: big ideas, past, present and future speculation, scientific and technological elements and a critical analysis of society. All of that in a condensed format, which is perhaps more consistent with the fast pace of present times. Let's hope that short fiction keeps doing this, and that many more markets take notice and participate in the renaissance of sci-fi and fantasy short fiction for it to keep growing those trees from Cortazar's quote: excellent fiction with the ability to transform us by its powerful imagination.

Acknowledgements

The first time *Alphaland* came to life in 2018, I wrote about authors not being islands and ended the book with a quote by Jean-François Lyotard: 'A self does not amount to much, but no self is an island; each exists in a fabric of relations that is now more complex and mobile than ever before.'

Today, I stand by this sentence more than ever. As creators of stories, we share time and space in a reality that is more unpredictable than ever. Now when uncertainty reigns, we are anchored through our relations with those around us, the ones we gravitate toward in our lows and highs, those who celebrate our achievements.

'You know who you are' is what normally we write here in the acknowledgmentsd but, let's be honest, you don't know. I have not thanked you in person, mainly because I live far, far away, in a land of sun and sand. So, you live your lives oblivious about how much you mean to me. You, Leticia, Miquel, Elías, Josep María, Pedro, Alicia, Nieves, Aritz, Carla and Lluis. You all, my beta readers, gave me strength when I lacked it. And you, Sue, Monica, James, Steve, Inés, the best translators anyone could ask for, believed in my stories. This book would never have been what it is without you.

You, Robert, a *maestro* with what I suspect are magical powers, took me under your wing and push me to fly. And again you, Marian, my editor, translator, writing buddy, literary ally, and fellow conspirator. Without your vision and support, this adventure would have stayed an impossible dream and not a mission accomplished.

And also, you, Mariana y Patricia, sisters in life and sisters in crime. Always with me in any circumstances.

And last but not least, you, Sam and Max, the light and the joy, and you, Omar, my beacon, my stronghold, my partner.

Each and every one of the stories in this collection took form because you were close, one way or another. I recognise your enthusiasm in each word and see you in the turns of each storyline. I hope you understand how important you are to me, how you make me feel like a part of an archipelago and how much I appreciate your existence.

Now, I hope you know.

This edition of
Alphaland and Other Tales
was sent to print
on 4 September 2023,
anniversary of the birth
of imaginative fantasist
Joan Aiken

CALQUE PRESS